HEART

GARRETT LEIGH

Second Edition ISBN: 9781913220068

Cover Art: Garrett Leigh @ blackjazzdesign.com

FOREWORD

This book was loosely based on events that took place a few miles from my home a number years before I wrote it. That said, it is a work of fiction and Dex's story is in no way representative of every Traveller.

Huge thanks to my sensitivity readers from way back when the first edition was published, and to John-jo for your wisdom and encouragement the second time round. Thank you from the bottom of my heart for letting me into your world.

CHAPTER ONE

Spring 2011

Seb Wright tugged off his bandana and pushed his dark, sweat-dampened hair away from his eyes. The thick, syrupy scent of vanilla hung heavy in the air. He was exhausted and in desperate need of a shave, but with the kitchen clean and the shop stocked, his workday had finally come to an end.

He put the last of his equipment away and wandered to the back area to wash up and get changed. His legs felt like lead and he considered making the five-minute walk home in his grubby chef whites, but tired as he was, a fudge-smeared pastry chef meandering through town in the middle of the night wasn't a good look for business.

Not that there was anyone around to see him. Yawning, he reached for his clothes and glanced through the window at the Cornish harbour town he called home. Padstow, Cornwall—population 3,162, according to Wikipedia, and in winter, he could believe it. Short, blustery days gave way to long, stormy nights when the sea lashed the harbour like a demon from the dark and there wasn't a soul to be seen outside.

In summer, though, it was a different world. The sea was calm and still and the streets became a riot of uncontainable energy.

Seb longed for and dreaded those days in equal measure. Longed for because it signalled the dreary austerity of winter was over, but dreaded because it meant the relentless chaos of the tourist season had begun. That was the problem with seasonal income: the fluctuation from one extreme to the other. His inherited artisan fudge pantry was one of a kind. When it did well, it thrived, but the long winter months were harsh, and this year, he couldn't wait to see the back of it.

In a daze, he walked home through the silent streets. It was long after midnight, and spring had been wet and quiet, but the weathermen promised an all too rare balmy British summer was just around the corner, and he needed to be ready. After a week of late nights, it seemed he finally was.

He turned onto one of the cobbled side streets that filtered off the main roads like estuaries. His cottage was right around the corner between a traditional pasty shop and a not-so-traditional den for henna tattoos. There was a scuffling noise behind him, but he paid it no heed. Walking around in the dead of night didn't bother him; it never had. He knew Padstow like the back of his hand. He'd grown up here, and after working in London through most of his twenties, he'd found his way back to the family business like a good local boy. It would take more than a cat rifling through bins to make him look around.

He continued on his way, fantasising about the extra-large beers stashed in his fridge. His stomach growled. He'd eaten nothing but tastings from pots of warm fudge all day, and he knew the girls from the pasty shop would've saved him some leftovers. Only appendicitis and the worst hangover in the world had ever dulled his appetite for the pasties Gem and her girls had been baking in Padstow for as long as he could remember.

Seb stopped under the streetlamp by the chip shop and pulled out his wallet. The girls in the pasty shop never let him pay for his dinner, but he always slipped a fiver through the letterbox anyway. Winters in Cornwall were hard, and they all needed every penny.

He found his wallet surprisingly well stocked until he remembered his planned predawn trip to the dairy farm in the morning. He suppressed a sigh and shoved his wallet in his back pocket. The farm was a fifteen-mile round trip in a borrowed car, and with the supermarket just a mile up the road, supporting local businesses was a pain in the arse.

That's what you get for having pretentious organic principles.

Seb gave his quasi older brother a mental eye roll. Then the wind from the ocean picked up and whistled through the narrow street. He shivered. The cold didn't usually bother him. He glanced around, rubbing his arms. Was it his imagination, or did the shadows seem darker than usual?

He shook himself, amused at his ominous train of thought. *That's what you get for working eighteen hours four days straight. Man up, you daft twat.*

Still, he found himself glancing over his shoulder anyway.

One of the shadows moved. He was sure of it. The dark shape seemed to dance across the narrow street with the same scuffling noise he'd heard before. He froze. The hair on the back of his neck stood on end. His breath caught and his heart thumped, and all at once, he knew he wasn't alone.

Seb shook his head and turned away, searching out the peeling white paint of his front door. He was tired, that was all, so tired he was imagining shit that wasn't there. It was a shame he wasn't delirious or drunk instead. The fun he could have with that....

Unbidden, he remembered when he'd last brought a companion back to this very street the previous summer. They'd barely made it to his tiny backyard, where he'd let Carlos the Portuguese fisherman fuck him over the back wall. Clichéd? Maybe, but it had been bloody good. He wondered absently if the *Angelina* was heading back to the West Coast this year.

A cool hand clamped down on Seb's shoulder.

"What the—" He whirled around, his heart in his mouth. "What the fuck?"

The owner of the hand took a step back. "You dropped your wallet."

"What?" Seb sucked in a much-needed gulp of air, hoping the

stranger with the soft Irish brogue couldn't hear the thundering stampede of his heart, or the stupidity in his moronic one-word response.

"Your wallet," the stranger repeated, holding out his hand, a slight smirk colouring what Seb was fast realizing was a beautiful face. "You dropped it by the chip shop."

Seb took the wallet and shoved it into his back pocket. "Thanks."

"You're welcome."

The stranger started to turn away. Seb caught his arm. "Wait."

The street was dark, lit only by a single street lamp, but even in the dim light, Seb could see the boy was blond, really blond, and his shrewd eyes were wide and light. Grey, maybe. His features were angled and perfectly proportioned, and his frame was lean… too lean. Closer inspection revealed tatty, dirty clothes and a frayed, holey rucksack slung over his shoulder.

The stranger was a vagrant. *Bloody hell. He's one of the tramps from behind the docks.*

Even as the thought crossed Seb's mind, it seemed somehow wrong to brand the beautiful boy with such ugly words. Not many tourists knew about the small crowd of homeless people who populated Padstow in the warmer months. They touted for work during the day and slept by the water at night. It was a side of the affluent portside town most visitors never saw.

Even Seb had never seen *his* face before. "How old are you?"

"What?" The stranger raised an insolent eyebrow.

Seb ignored the tingle of energy the gesture evoked. "You look too young to be out on the streets at this time of night."

"I'm twenty-two."

Seb frowned before he could stop himself. Twenty-two? Fat chance. Seb was twenty-six, and there was no way just four years separated him from the slender youngster, but even as he processed the thought, the stranger was on the move again. He pulled his arm from Seb's grasp, and this time, he was gone before Seb could formulate a response.

Did that really just happen? As Seb drifted the last twenty meters or so to his cottage, retrieved his dinner from the shop next door, and paid for it, he wasn't entirely sure.

CHAPTER TWO

THE FOLLOWING morning, Seb woke gasping for breath and drenched in sweat, dragged from a haunting dream of a platinum-haired presence in his bed, writhing beneath him. The encounter had felt surreal, like the young man in his bed was a ghost, but it was hot as hell. He looked down at his still-hard dick and groaned aloud. Christ, he hadn't had dreams like that since he'd watched Carlos sail away from him nearly a year ago, and even *those* dreams hadn't been quite like the one still lingering in his sleep-clouded brain. It had been years since he'd wanted to top anyone, much less fantasized about it. And since when had dirty dreams become so poetic?

He lay still for a moment, listening to the seagulls call good morning to each other, and considered taking himself in hand. Considered letting his eyes close and drifting back to white-blond hair, pale skin, and the earth-moving sex he'd dreamed about.

"For God's sake, man, just get up."

There was no one around to hear his grumble save his elderly cat, Esme, who offered him a waspish stare from the windowsill. Barely dawn it may have been, but his feline companion was an early riser, and it was clear by her scowl she'd been waiting on him awhile.

Seb rolled from the bed and wandered into the bathroom,

yawning and scratching his belly. He stepped under the tepid shower, washing the sweat of his imaginary amorous night away, and once dressed, he ambled downstairs to feed Esme.

At the kitchen sink, he stared through the window at his limited view of the sea. The sun was out, bright and bold, and the air was distinctly muggy, at least muggy for a late-May morning. Perhaps for once his luck was in, and summer had indeed come early.

After breakfast, he made his way to the shop, noting the streets seemed busier already, even at the arse crack of dawn. He let himself in to Alfie's, named after his great-grandfather, who'd founded the business in 1929, and went straight to the computer, booted it up, and checked for overnight Internet orders.

There were a few. He boxed them up while drinking a cup of strong builder's tea and left them in the office for Nicole, his single permanent employee, to post on her lunch break. After that, he set about replenishing the specialty flavours the display counter was running low on. Coffee and rum first, then the newfangled salted caramel he was still on the fence about.

He saved the traditional vanilla to make later, when the shop was open. It was part of the charm of Alfie's—the fudge being made in the shop window—and he'd being doing it since he was ten years old. These days, he didn't notice the faces pressed to the glass or the people milling around him, but all the same, it was far less hassle to get the complicated flavours out of the way while he had some time to himself.

The fudge making process came to him as naturally as breathing, swirling the butter and sugar in a pan that was older than he was, pushing the finished fudge around on the cooling slab until it was ready to set and be cut. Most days, he thought he could make fudge in his sleep. Some days, he probably did, especially in the summertime.

Nicole joined him around ten, and at midday, he left her assembling gift boxes and took a break. He wandered down to the waterfront and bought a crab sandwich from the wooden shack whose owner had seen the same promise in the weather he had and opened his doors early.

He sat on the big stone wall by the boats and ate his lunch. When he was done, he cast his gaze around the bustling seafront. It wasn't anywhere near as busy as it was going to get come July, but there was still an undeniable shift in the air, an energy that would remain until the middle of September. Even the casual tourist stalls were already set up down by the small sandy beach and open for business—the candy floss, the popcorn, the fake tattoos, and hair braiding….

Wait.

Seb swivelled back to the hair-braiding stand. The vendor was engrossed in weaving brightly coloured thread into the long hair of a wriggling child, head down, eyes down, but even with his face hidden, the shock of white-blond hair was unmistakable. Seb twisted farther round to get a better look, taking in the thin, undernourished arms and the pale skin he'd hardly seen in the dark of their midnight encounter.

It was him, it had to be.

As though he could feel eyes on him, the young man glanced up. For a moment, it felt like his fathomless grey gaze locked with Seb's, but in reality, Seb knew it was unlikely the lad had noticed his lone figure sitting on the portside so far away.

Seb stared at him far longer than he should have, and long after the man had turned his attention back to his work. For some reason, he was strangely reassured the beautiful young vagrant had found himself a job. At a couple of quid a pop, braiding children's hair wouldn't pay much, but it would at least buy him a hot dinner every night.

Or the drug to feed whatever addiction has him out on the streets….

Seb silenced the judgmental monster in his brain by getting to his feet and dusting crumbs from his worn-out jeans. Growing up as the token gay in a small, traditional town had taught him harsh stereotyping ruined lives, and somehow, Seb knew the young blond deserved better than that.

IN TYPICAL British style, the warm weather didn't hold, but it lasted long enough to keep Seb busy. In recent years, that seemed to be the trick with the fickle Cornish summer: start off with a golden blaze of clear blue skies and end with a damp, grey squib.

It was the middle of June when the weather took a turn for the worse. It wasn't all that cold, but it was wet, and the wind sweeping in from the Atlantic Ocean was vicious without the sun to temper it.

The chilly snap made Seb think of his parents enjoying their retirement in sunny Spain, but more often than he cared to admit, he found himself wondering about the mysterious blond vagrant. He caught sight of him on the beach from time to time, so he knew he was still around selling hair braiding, and by the look of him, sleeping rough down by the water.

One blustery Saturday evening, Seb closed the shop and paused a moment before turning to face the music. After one of the busiest days of the year so far, the place was a mess. The weekend staff had left for the day and Nicole had dashed off early to deal with a family crisis, so he knew he was in for a long night if the place was to be ready for another crazy day.

Seb opened the fridge. If he was tackling this bombsite alone, he needed a beer, but the shelves were bare. Cursing, he pulled a hoodie on over his grubby chef whites and braved the rain to run to the off-license a few streets away.

He was on his way back with a four-pack of Stella when he spotted the young blond. He was sheltering in the doorway of the beachwear shop across the street from Alfie's and didn't seem especially worried that he was already soaked to the skin.

Something pulled at Seb's chest. It took just a few seconds to decide to cross the street, and less than that to actually do it. He was on top of the vagrant before he realised he hadn't planned what to say. "Er, remember me?"

The blond raised a lazy eyebrow and ran his inscrutable gaze over Seb. "Should I?"

"You rescued my wallet a few weeks back."

Recognition coloured the young man's features; recognition and an infinitesimal shade of suspicion. "I didn't take anything from it."

Seb held up his hands in a placating gesture. "I know. I wanted to say thanks, and see if you wanted to come inside and get out of this rain."

"Inside? Like, *in* your shop?"

Seb jerked his head toward Alfie's. "Yep. That's it, right there. I'm going to be there awhile cleaning up. You're welcome to come in and dry off for a bit."

For a moment, the young man stared at him like he'd grown two heads, and then a shiver passed through him, and he shrugged with an indifference that couldn't be faked. "Okay."

Seb led the way around to the back door. Once inside, he rooted out a towel and tossed it the young man's way. "What's your name?"

"Why?" The question was flat, but the young man's face was hidden by the towel as he rubbed it over his hair, and Seb couldn't see if he was offended or not.

"Why not? Is it a secret?"

"No, it's Dex."

Seb filled the kettle. "Dex? Short for Dexter?"

"No, just Dex."

Seb turned the name over in his mind. *Dex. Dex. Dex.* It seemed to suit the enigmatic young blond, though he couldn't say why.

"Is your name Alfie?"

Seb swallowed a laugh. "No, that was my great-granddad. I'm Seb."

Dex smirked. "Sebastian?"

"Only my mum calls me that. Do you want a brew?"

Dex lowered the towel and folded it into a neat square. "No, it's okay. I should probably be going."

"It's still pissing down out there." Seb pointed to the window.

"Stay, it's no worries. I've got lots to do, anyway. Are you hungry?"

Dex glanced around, taking in the mess of a chaotic day. "For fudge? Doesn't look like you've got much left."

"I have more in the storeroom, but no, I meant real food. I can make you a sandwich, and I think I have some crisps somewhere."

Seb rummaged in the cupboard beside the fridge without waiting for an answer. He could tell Dex wanted to say no, but at the same time, the kid was hungry. He had to be. No one got that thin on three square meals a day.

He unearthed a multipack of Hula Hoops and slid them across the counter. "There you go. I'll make you a butty. Cheese and pickle do you?"

Dex pulled a face that made him look even younger than the twenty-two years he claimed to be. "Have you got Marmite?"

As it turned out, Seb did. He shoved his forgotten beer into the fridge and set to work making sandwiches for them both. When he was done, he brewed mugs of hot, sweet tea. Both sandwiches were gone by the time he turned around.

He suppressed a smile, knowing Dex wouldn't take kindly to being ribbed, and watched with amusement as Dex absently slid a Hula Hoop onto the end of each finger. It was an endearing, childish thing to do, and he found himself fascinated.

To break the spell, he picked up his cooling mug of tea. "I'm going out front to clear up. Help yourself to anything you want."

As he left the room, he pondered the sanity of leaving a vagrant unattended, especially one with the rough lilt of a Traveller accent, but he couldn't bring himself to go back and watch over Dex. Something inexplicable told him to give the kid some space, and that's just what he did.

Later, when the shop was in some sort of order, he came back to the kitchen to find Dex with his hands in the sink. Around him was a whole day's worth of used equipment, clean and stacked, ready to be put away.

"I didn't know where to put it," he offered by way of explanation.

Seb raised an eyebrow, running his gaze over the spotless kitchen. Dex had probably saved him another two hours of work. "You didn't have to do that."

Dex dried his hands on a tea towel and averted his eyes. "That's how it works, isn't it? You don't get nothing for free."

"You gave me my wallet back."

Dex shrugged. "And you gave me shelter from the storm."

CHAPTER THREE

OVER THE next few weeks, they fell into a strange kind of routine. Seb would send Nicole home early and shut the shop alone, all the while waiting for the tentative knock at the back door that signalled Dex was done for the day too.

Dex ate everything Seb put in front of him and scrubbed every pot he could find. He didn't say much, but Seb didn't mind that. The youngster didn't waste his words, and he possessed a caustic wit that made Seb laugh. His quiet company was more than worth the price of a bland sandwich and a safe place to eat.

The extra pair of hands was useful too, though Dex never ventured to the front of the shop. Civilized he may have been, but he still looked—and smelled—like the vagrant he was. Instead, when he was done with the cleaning, he invariably turned his hand to packing up the Internet orders Seb had let slide, and it fast became clear he was far better at folding gift boxes and tying ribbons than Seb was, something that didn't go unnoticed by Nicole.

"Is it me, or are you getting much better at this?" she said one day, holding a box up to the light. "Your boxes usually look like a five-year-old packed them."

Seb scowled but averted his gaze. He'd neglected to tell Nicole about his regular evening visitor. In fact, he hadn't told anyone about Dex at all. Distracted, he glanced at the clock. It was nearing 5:30 p.m. and closing time. Time for Nicole to leave and Dex to arrive. Without answering her question, he sent her home and locked the front door, trying to ignore the familiar bubble of excitement in the pit of his stomach.

Because, vagrant or not, and despite Dex's often sullen silence, there was no denying the growing attraction Seb felt. His shock of angelic hair, his shrewd, intelligent eyes. Even his grubby, nail-bitten hands haunted Seb's dreams.

Sometimes he thought he imagined the invisible current between them. The half smiles, the lingering looks. The zap of energy when their hands brushed. Other days, he allowed himself to become convinced Dex felt it too. After all, it wasn't the crappy sandwiches that kept him coming back. It couldn't be. No one liked Marmite *that* much. Seb drifted to the kitchen to make Dex's supper and wondered how he'd feel today.

And wondered, and wondered, as, long after the shop was clean and ready for the next day, the sandwich and obligatory bag of Hula Hoops lay on the counter, untouched.

For the first time in weeks, Dex hadn't stopped by.

Seb hung around at the shop, stretching out jobs that didn't need doing, buying time before he called it quits and went home. But he couldn't relax. Time ticked by and the hour got later, and when daylight faded around nine, he admitted defeat and decamped to the pub at the end of the street.

He felt better with a pint of ale in his restless hands, but the gnawing worry in his belly was persistent. He thought over the last few times he'd seen Dex. Had anything been different? Had he given any indication he was in trouble or going to skip town? He mulled it over until his second pint was done and his brain hurt, but he discovered no clue as to where Dex might be.

It was close to eleven when he slid from his bar stool to go home. He was tired and more than a little tipsy, and it was only by chance that he caught the conversation going on between two elderly local tradesmen at the end of the bar.

"Awful business," Jonah, the butcher, said. "And in front of all those kids too. The coppers turned up eventually, but of course, they were all gone by then. They always are."

"That's what happens when you let the gypos in," the other man chimed in. "I said this would happen when they built that site down at Redruth."

"That's thirty miles away," Seb said. "What's that got to do with here?"

The old men glanced up, noticing him for the first time. "They're spreading out," Jonah said darkly. "And they're bringing their trouble with them. There was about ten of them brawling on the beach this afternoon, fighting over those little stalls of crap. Animals, they are, scrapping over a few quid."

Seb refrained from pointing out a few quid to one man was everything to another. "Which stalls were they fighting over?"

"All of 'em, as far as we could tell. They kicked seven bells out of one poor kid. He got away, but I doubt he got far."

Seb's heart began a slow, insistent tattoo in his ears. They were talking about Dex, they had to be. There were five stalls down on the beachfront—two were run by women, and the other two by older, homeless men. Jonah and his friend were old, but even through their faded eyes, Dex was the only vendor who could be described as a kid. "When did this happen?"

The old men looked his way again, startled, like they'd long forgotten the conversation and were talking about something else. "This afternoon," Jonah said. "But don't you worry yourself, laddie. That kind of scum sticks to the beach and the street carts. They won't come near your fancy shop."

Seb was halfway to the door by then and didn't bother to reply. He stepped out onto the street and spun in a slow circle. Dex was in trouble, of that there was no doubt, but he didn't have a clue what to do about it. He had no idea where Dex slept at night, no idea where he called home, and certainly no idea where he would go if he was hurt or scared.

He looked everywhere he could think of: the beach, the harbour, and the back alleys. He even braved a trip to the disused boat dock, but the leery, threatening stares of the drunks and junkies sheltering there drove him back.

Eventually, he ran out of ideas and trudged home with a heavy heart. Dex could've been anywhere. Perhaps he'd even fled the town, or worse, his attackers, whoever they were, had caught up with him and finished the job.

He drifted back through the deserted streets in a horrified, nauseous daze, and was halfway home before it occurred to him to check the shop one more time. As far as he knew, it was the only safe place Dex knew in Padstow. It was worth another look, wasn't it?

Even in the darkness, from fifty feet away, he detected the shape of Dex huddled in a ball by the back door.

He broke into a run and dropped to the ground beside him. "Dex? You all right?"

It took some persuasion, but Dex raised his head and met his gaze. Seb was horrified. Dex's beautiful pale face was bloody and bruised, one of his eyes completely swollen shut.

"Bloody hell. You should go to A and E."

Dex shook his head. "No. No hospitals. Just need a… plaster or something."

It was going to take more than a box of Elastoplast to heal the wounds on his face, but without a car, Seb had no way of taking him to the nearest hospital. Somehow, he knew Dex wouldn't wait around if he called an ambulance.

"Come inside."

His tone left no room for argument, and for once, none was forthcoming from Dex. He let Seb help him to his feet before he walked inside of his own volition and all but fell onto the countertop stool Seb thought of as his.

Seb fetched the rudimentary first-aid kit from the bathroom. There wasn't much to it, just antiseptic and dressings, but it would have to do. He cleaned the injuries he could see. When he was done, Dex looked marginally better, though the bruising to his face still worried Seb.

"Did they knock you out?"

"No. It was nothing, really. Just a scuffle."

Seb frowned. "About what?"

"Territory."

"Territory?"

Dex lifted his gaze from the countertop and shrugged. "Yeah. They want to put one of their own on all the carts. I think today was a warning to my boss."

Seb reached out and touched Dex's swollen cheek. "What are you going to do?"

"Nothing." Dex shrugged again. "My boss won't care. All he wants is his money. He won't be scared of skanks like that. It's all part of the game."

Seb was lost, but he knew one thing for certain: he didn't want Dex used as a pawn in *any* game, especially one as violent as this turf war appeared to be. "Can't you do something else?"

"Like what?"

"You could work for me."

Dex snorted and slid from his stool. "And be your bitch? No, thanks."

Seb caught his arm as he turned away. Dex winced and pulled back, clearly more hurt than he wanted to let on.

"That's not what I meant," Seb said, though he wasn't entirely sure what he *did* mean. "I just… I worry about you out there, and I like having you around the shop. I missed you tonight."

Dex's expression softened, though the glare in his one working eye remained, mutinous and stubborn. "I don't want your charity. I don't want that from you."

CHAPTER FOUR

SEB STIRRED a thick, sludgy pan of chocolate fudge, distracted by a head full of Dex. It had been a week since he'd discovered Dex bloody and bruised on his doorstep, and even after all that had happened, there was only one thing on his mind.

"I don't want that from you."

As Seb stirred the precarious molten mix in the pan, the softly uttered words swirled around his brain, drowned out only by the question he'd failed to ask at the time.

So what do you want from me, Dex?

Not that he'd have gotten an answer. Soon after that particular discussion, Dex had refused his platonic offer of a couch to kip on and disappeared into the night. Seb hadn't held out much hope of him appearing for his supper the following night, but he had, and he'd turned up like clockwork every night since, keeping his reluctant promise to check in every day. There had been no further incidents down at the beach either, though Dex remained defiant he wasn't giving up his stall for anyone.

The smell of burning sugar brought Seb out of his daydreams. He looked down at the smoking pan and swore, startling the last few customers milling around the shop. He muttered a contrite apology as he took the pan from the heat and turned the flame off. Chocolate fudge was tricky and required concentration, something he seemed to be lacking today.

He took the pan to the back, dumped its contents in the bin, and filled it with water, hoping to soak off the worst of the damage. Catering-sized copper-based pans were expensive, and he could do without having to replace one.

Sighing, he retrieved a fresh pan and slung it onto the back-room stove, effectively confining himself to the kitchen for the rest of the day. He didn't have the patience for any more public mistakes.

Weighing the ingredients by eye, he prepared a fresh pan and attempted to fire up the hob. Nothing happened. He tried again, and again, and even tried the stove in the shop, but both hobs remained cold and unlit.

Brilliant. It was Friday night, the shelves were bare, and the bloody gas was out. He swore again. There was nothing for it; he would have to gather his equipment and take his work home to his tiny ceramic oven.

He was on his third trip between the cottage and the shop when the heavens opened. He couldn't believe his rotten luck, until he spotted Dex shuffling up the street, once again soaked to the skin.

For a moment, he stared. The bruises on Dex's face had faded to a dull shade of greenish yellow, and from a distance, they could hardly be seen. The image of him huddled in the doorway of the beachwear shop flashed into his mind, and Seb found himself suddenly, irrationally furious.

Were they really still there? Really still in a place where Dex was hiding from a summer storm with nowhere to go? Still in a place where Seb went home to his comfortable bed every night with no clue where Dex laid his head?

Hell no.

Something inside him snapped. He propped the heavy cooling slab he carried against a dry stone wall, pulled his hood up, and started down the road.

"Come home with me."

Dex blinked. "What?"

"Come home with me. You can't sleep out in this."

"Says who?"

The defiance in Dex's eyes broke Seb's heart. Dex had never admitted he had no place to call home, and it seemed he never would. "Says me," Seb snapped. "I'm working at home tonight, and you're coming with me."

Dex stared at him, his face inscrutable, and the silence stretched on and on, punctuated only by a brutal clap of thunder. "What do you want from me?"

Seb stepped closer and touched the fading marks on Dex's face. "I want you to be safe and dry, even if it's only for one night. I can't... fuck. I can't leave you out here. Please don't make me."

He expected a fight, stubborn resistance, or even downright rejection, but Dex had been surprising him since the night he'd stepped out of the shadows and into his life.

Dex shrugged and shifted his ever-present backpack to his other shoulder. "All right, all right. You don't have to drag me. I'm coming."

Seb hadn't realised he'd grabbed the sleeves of Dex's tatty sweatshirt. Startled, he let go. "Really? You'll come with me?"

"Said I would, didn't I?"

Seb had no answer for that. Instead, he turned and dashed back to his abandoned stack of equipment, trusting Dex would follow.

He did, and though he seemed a little confused by the task, he helped Seb hoof the remainder of the equipment back to the cottage.

Once inside, he seemed a little lost... lost and *wet*. They'd both been caught in the rain, but it was obvious Dex had been out in it far longer than Seb. Chances were the cottage was the first time he'd been indoors since he'd had supper at the shop the previous night.

Seb kicked off his trainers and opened the cupboard under the stairs. He found a clean towel and tossed it to Dex. "Go take a hot shower. I'll find you some clothes."

Dex glanced toward the steep stairs of the cottage. "You want me to go upstairs in your house?"

"Bathroom is first door on the right."

Seb headed for the kitchen without waiting for a response. He felt better having Dex safe in his home, but that didn't change the fact that he had twenty kilos of fudge to make before morning.

He was on the first batch of the last flavour, vanilla, when Dex reappeared, dressed in the tracksuit bottoms and T-shirt Seb had left for him on the landing. The clothes were huge on him, clinging to his slender frame and highlighting the protruding bones of his hips and shoulders, but without the perpetual layer of dirt, Dex's pale skin seemed to shimmer in the fading light of the day. With his damp hair sticking up and out in every direction, it was a startling combination.

With considerable effort, Seb tore his gaze away and focused on the pan of bubbling fudge. He didn't have time to make any more mistakes, and he didn't look up as Dex skulked to the sink and slipped seamlessly into his well-practiced role of cleaning up Seb's mess.

They worked in companionable silence for an hour or so. Esme appeared at some point and watched them suspiciously from the cardboard box she'd claimed on top of the fridge. When the last batch of molten fudge reached the perfect soft-ball temperature, Seb poured it onto the marble cooling slab and pushed it around with the wooden paddle. The rhythm of the task was soothing and the one part of his job he found vaguely relaxing.

He'd fairly dropped off the face of the earth by the time he became aware of Dex beside him, closer than he'd ever been before.

"All right?"

Dex peered at the cooling slab. "Why are you doing that?"

"To cool it down so it sets. Then I can cut it."

"It smells nice." Dex sniffed the air. The sweet, buttery scent of vanilla seemed to travel through his lean frame. "It smells like you."

Seb smiled, remembering Dex had never seen the fudge being made before, just the messy aftermath. "Want to taste it?"

"Really?"

Seb swiped his work-hardened index finger through the still-hot fudge and held it out. "Here you go."

He expected Dex to take the fudge from him with his newly clean thumb. The last thing he expected was the slippery heat of his tongue.

Dex sucked Seb's finger into his mouth and swirled away every trace of fudge before he drew back. "Doesn't taste like the purple one."

Seb snorted, ignoring the warmth stirring in his groin. "Cadbury's? That's because this is the proper old-fashioned stuff, handmade with real ingredients, not chemical crap."

"How long have you been making it?"

"Me? My whole bloody life, but my family has been making this recipe since the twenties."

"That's nice," Dex said absently, his reflective gaze still on the fudge Seb had started pushing around again.

Seb pondered the brooding haze that had suddenly descended over Dex's pensive eyes. Bad memories? Or good ones that seemed too far away? Whatever it was, it made him want to take Dex in his arms and hold him until the sadness was gone forever.

Instead, he held out the wooden paddle. "Want a go?"

It took some silent persuasion, but eventually Dex took the paddle from him and tried his hand at pushing the cooling fudge around the marble slab. He did a fine job at first, but as the fudge cooled and thickened, it became harder to handle, and he didn't have the strength in his undernourished arms.

Against his better judgment, Seb reached around and closed his hands over Dex's. Dex faltered a moment before he let out a shaky breath and resumed the motion of manipulating the fudge.

It was a few minutes before Seb realised the effect Dex's close proximity was having on him. The way they stood, pressed together with Dex all but enveloped in his arms, left Dex's hair

22

tickling his face and the bare skin of his pale neck just inches away.

Before he could stop, he leaned closer and inhaled the clean scent of Dex's freshly washed skin. He smelled like Seb's minty shower gel and shampoo, mixed with a natural, musky scent that smelled like the earth.

Dex leaned back against him, arching his neck to give him better access.

Fudge forgotten, Seb kissed the soft skin of Dex's pale white throat, tentatively at first, then with more purpose as Dex let go of the paddle and sucked in a sharp breath.

He should stop, he knew he should stop, but somehow the voice of reason faded away to nothing as he supported Dex's slim frame and absorbed the warmth from his body.

Dex remained silent and pliant in his arms, the only sign he was enjoying Seb's attentions the subtle, rhythmic roll of his hips. Then he shuddered and let out a breathless moan, slumping forward and dropping his hands to the kitchen counter, the motion pushing his lower body back into Seb's groin. "Oh God, oh God. I didn't come here for this."

Seb got ahold of himself and loosened his grip. "It's not why I asked you to come, I swear."

Dex caught him as he moved away. "Don't stop. Please."

Perhaps it was the plaintive edge to his voice, or the simple fact that he was begging for something Seb had been craving for months, but a heartbeat later, something exploded between them.

Seb pulled Dex to him and kissed him. Dex fell slack in his arms and kissed him back with a ferocity that belied his slim, fragile frame.

They tore at each other's clothes. Dex's slipped easily away from him and revealed a number of boot-shaped imprints on his back that stopped Seb in his tracks.

"What the—?"

Dex cut him off with another crazed kiss. "Don't look at them."

He shoved at Seb's underwear and took his hard, aching dick

in his hand. With just a tiny flick of his wrist, he had Seb's mind devoid of anything but being naked and desperate in the vanilla-scented heat of his kitchen.

Seb fumbled for the lube and condoms hidden fortuitously in a kitchen drawer from Carlos's last visit. He shook one out. "Top or bottom?"

The question seemed to confuse Dex. He stared at the condom before pushing it away and back toward Seb's cock.

Top it is, then.

It suited Seb… felt right. He usually bottomed, but with Dex, he wanted to be inside him, to possess every inch of his fragile body.

Dex groaned and turned in his arms, leaning over the counter again. "Do it. I want you to fuck me."

Seb knew all too well the pain and discomfort caused by a careless and inconsiderate top, so, despite the wild heat between them, he took a moment to prepare Dex for him, stretching him with his fingers, then easing his condom-covered cock in slow and gentle, inch by inch.

The pedestrian pace killed him, but it was Dex who ran out of patience first. He tightened his grip on the countertop and slammed his hips back, taking Seb all the way into him in a single, brutal thrust.

Seb gasped, absorbing the smooth heat of Dex tight around him. It had been… fuck, he didn't even know how long it had been since he'd been inside another man. He'd forgotten what it felt like. How dizzying and consuming it was. "Easy," he got out through stuttered breaths. "Am I hurting you?"

"No. God no. Don't stop."

Seb pulled out and pushed in again, and shuddered as a bolt of sensation tore through him. His shaking hands seemed huge around Dex's slender hips, like the paws of an animal on its prey, but he couldn't control the ever tightening, bruising grip.

Dex shuddered and arched his back. "*Oh.*"

Seb froze. Déjà vu swept over him. He looked down at Dex's pale, bruised back, at his protruding hips and halo of white-gold hair, struck by a sudden, overwhelming certainty they'd done this before.

He faltered. No. That wasn't possible. He'd never even seen Dex until he'd crept up on Seb that dark, dark night. Had he?

He wanted to laugh when he remembered the dirty dream he'd had that night and many nights after. Had it really been so long that he was confusing his wet dreams with reality?

But he didn't laugh. He didn't laugh, because once again, Dex got tired of waiting and took matters into his own hands.

Dex came upright and looped one arm around Seb's neck, pulling him down for a fierce kiss. "Stop bloody thinking and fuck me."

Seb didn't need telling twice. He pushed Dex forward and slammed into him.

Dex cried out and widened his legs to steady himself.

His head hung low, his breath raw, ragged gasps. His legs shook, and before long, Seb was bearing the burden of holding them both up.

Seb bent and ran his tongue over Dex's bruised back. It felt so good to be buried inside him. Too good, and for a moment, he was almost afraid, like the punch line was going to hit him way too hard.

Then Dex clenched around him and came in his hand, convulsing like he'd been hit by a train, and coherent thought abandoned him.

Seb chased his own orgasm as Dex slumped forward, spent. It was close, closer than he thought, and it roared through him and knocked him off-balance. As he groaned and pressed his face between Dex's sweat-slicked shoulder blades, only Dex's perilous grip on the counter kept them both upright.

CHAPTER FIVE

SEB RECOVERED first. He peeled himself from Dex's back and pulled out of him. Dex made a small, breathless noise of discontent. Seb grabbed a roll of kitchen paper, disposed of the condom, and wiped his hands. He was sated, and he'd come harder than he had in years, but the sense that his job wasn't done niggled at him.

Gently, he roused Dex and pried his hands from the counter. "Come upstairs."

He led Dex by the hand to his bedroom, and together, they fell onto the unmade bed and kissed until Seb found more lube and another condom. In the dim light of the room, he hooked Dex's legs over his shoulders and slid into him again. Dex was only half-hard, but he pulled Seb over him and braced himself against the metal bedframe.

It didn't take long for things to unravel again, and for a while, the only sounds in the room were the squeak of the bedsprings and the brutal thump of the metal frame hitting the wall. Orgasm hit Seb first this time. Sweat dripped down his chest and he came with a strangled shout. Beneath him, Dex arched his back, clawing at Seb, his eyes still wild and wanting, but he didn't come.

Seb pulled out and took Dex in his mouth. Dex jumped, startled. Seb soothed him. He wanted Dex to feel as amazing as he did.

It didn't take long. Orgasm seemed to take Dex by surprise, but Seb absorbed every jolt and shudder as he finished Dex off by hand. He often saw a cynicism in Dex that broke his heart, but like this, he almost looked innocent. Like he'd never felt anything like it.

Seb crawled up the bed, wiped Dex down, and pulled Dex tight against him. Dex was quiet, his laboured breaths panting in time with Seb's until he raised his head a little while later. "You made me come."

Seb caught the disbelief in his tone and cracked an eye open. "Isn't that the point?"

"I didn't mean to the first time, and I didn't expect you to…." Dex trailed off, like he thought he'd said too much.

Seb frowned and tightened his arms around him. "It wouldn't be good for me if you didn't come."

Dex didn't answer, and Seb wondered if he'd fallen asleep. Since the attack at the beach, he'd noticed signs of exhaustion in him—bloodshot eyes and sketchy concentration. He'd drifted back to his initial suspicions about drugs and addiction, but in the end, turned away from them. How many times had he looked at his own tired face and known all he needed was a good night's sleep?

He ran his fingers through Dex's sweat-dampened hair. "Can I ask you something?"

Dex raised his head again, his hawkish gaze more alert than it had been moments before. Was that suspicion, or just plain curiosity? "Go on."

"Where are you from?"

"Here and there."

"That's pretty vague."

"If you say so."

"Are you a Traveller?"

Dex shrugged. "Whatever you want to call it."

"Where's your family?"

"Somewhere else."

Seb let it go. Some may have found it odd he'd taken a virtual stranger into his bed, but it was no different than the casual sex he'd shared with Carlos. He'd known next to nothing about the Portuguese fisherman, and he'd never much cared.

But even as the thought crossed his mind, he knew he was wrong. Everything about this was different. Dex was different. He wanted to know everything about him, and at the same time, nothing at all, because he was afraid of what Dex might tell him.

He rolled onto his side, facing Dex, who seemed suddenly nervous. Seb reached out and drew him closer, mashing their hot, sticky bodies together again, and wrapped his arms around him in a bruising, suffocating embrace. "You're safe here," he said quietly. "For as long as you want to be."

Dex didn't answer with words. Instead, he ducked his head and pressed himself so tight against Seb it almost hurt. They had sex one more time after that despite Seb's concern that Dex had to be sore. He took Dex on his stomach this time, holding his arms over his head. It was slow and sweet, and Seb had barely pulled out before Dex was fast asleep.

Seb watched him for a while. In sleep, Dex appeared even younger than he did awake, and not for the first time, Seb felt an urge to protect sweep through him. He covered them both with the thin duvet he used in the summer months and stood guard over Dex until sleep came for him.

It was dark when he woke, but he knew without opening his eyes he was alone. He rolled from the bed and ran down the stairs, bare to the chilly night air, but the kitchen was empty, and he knew before he looked at the floor that Dex's borrowed clothes would be picked up and folded neatly on the countertop. He looked anyway, and he *was* surprised to see the abandoned batch of fudge from the night before cut into perfectly equal squares and packed in the delicate boxes.

Seb's chest hurt. A calling card or a good-bye? Either way, Dex was gone.

CHAPTER SIX

S<small>EB HAD</small> eyes like a stormy sea and dark, dark hair that curled damply behind his ears when he worked, cleaning up the kitchen at the shop, or tonight when he'd cooked up that huge pan of fudge at home.

Dex ran his fingers through Seb's hair and found a perfect curl. He wanted to stick his finger in it to see if it held him tight... tight enough to stay here forever, but he didn't. The night was fading away, and their time together had come to an end.

With a quiet sigh, Dex slid from the bed. It felt wrong to slip away from Seb while he slept, but awake, those blue eyes would break Dex in a heartbeat. Blue eyes, warm arms, and a gentle smile. God, it would be so easy to stay here forever.

But they didn't have forever. The old world was calling Dex home, and he had to go. He pressed his lips to the pulse point in Seb's neck.

I'll never forget you.

Autumn 2012

D<small>EX CURLED</small> up in the corner of the drafty caravan. It was late, well after midnight, but for him, the night had only just begun.

He pulled his coat tighter around him. In his hand, he clutched a pay-as-you-go phone, waiting for it to ring and a creepy voice to lure him out into the night with the promise of clammy hands and putrid breath. He shivered. The caravan was filthy and cold but, as his master liked to remind him, it was out of the heavy rain lashing the single window.

Dex closed his eyes and attempted sleep, knowing the buzz of the phone would wake him before long, but it was no good. Even alone and away from the rough hands of his keeper, he couldn't find rest. Instead, he let his mind wander back in time to a summer he'd never forget, to those few short months that felt like a dream. Away from the Traveller sites, he'd been left to fend for himself, his only tie to hand his takings through the window of a dirty white van at the end of each day. Sleeping alone on the beach, without the weight of a dirty, stinking body over him, he'd had the time of his life.

And Seb. God, Seb. Some nights, Dex dreamed of him, but not of his face, or his body. No. The nights Seb came to Dex, he never saw him… never saw those deep blue eyes. Instead, he felt only the warmth of his touch seeping into his bones until he forgot what it was like to be cold. So cold his teeth ached.

The phone rang. Dex peered at the screen, though what he expected to see, he wasn't quite sure. Only one number called the phone he was given to hold every night. He pressed the call button. "Yeah?"

His "Uncle" Braden growled, "Get out here. You've got a job."

A job. Even in Braden's thick brogue, it sounded almost respectable. Shame it couldn't be farther from the truth.

Dex sloped across the muddy yard and got into the waiting van. Mikey, his driver for tonight and every night, turned to him with a leer. "You ready to get fucked, ya little poof?"

Dex ignored him and stared out the window, watching the site he called home roll by until they hit the brightly lit streets of Hatfield. Mikey's words were crude and cruel, but they were true. Dex worked the fairgrounds from time to time, but his main contribution to the "family" business was this: getting fucked by dirty old men. There was more money in hooking than all Braden's other enterprises combined, and Dex was a popular whore.

Fucking. Sucking. Sometimes a beating, but he took it all with little resistance. What was the point? He'd had a glimpse of another life, but it wasn't for him. He didn't belong in a world so free and beautiful.

Mikey drove to an estate on the outskirts of Hatfield. He pulled up by a block of flats and pushed Dex into the passenger door. "Flat Six. You've got thirty minutes, lad. Don't be late."

Dex slithered out of the van and drifted to the exterior door of the flats. He didn't have to turn to know Mikey was watching his every move, ready to drive over him if he put a foot out of place.

Don't you run, boyo. We'll always find you, and you know what happens to little boys who run.

The door to the flats was open. Dex let himself inside and paused, checking his pockets for his kit. Braden didn't believe in creature comforts for his "employee," and he didn't give two shits what happened behind closed doors, but perhaps because he was partial to sampling his own wares, he kept Dex supplied with condoms and lube.

Dex found the right door and knocked. An overweight middle-aged man answered, already half-undressed and sweating. Dex didn't take much notice as he followed him into the musty flat. After a while, they all looked the same.

"Do I have to pay extra to kiss you?"

Dex unzipped his thin coat. He knew he should say yes, that Braden would be pleased if he came back with extra cash, but he couldn't do it. Johns didn't usually want to kiss, and he'd only ever kissed one man for pleasure. "I don't kiss."

The man accepted it without complaint. Perhaps Dex had visited him before. He honestly couldn't remember. "Where do you want me?"

"On the couch," the man said. "I want you to suck me."

And so it went on, but as nights went, it turned out to be a pretty easy one—a run of blowjobs, hand jobs, and just one fucking from a john with a cock inadequate enough to cause a little discomfort.

Around dawn, Mikey drove Dex back to the site and ditched him outside Braden's plush mobile home. The site was a dump, but not Braden's place. He was the kingpin, and for him, no expense was spared.

Dex trudged up the steps, but before he could knock, Braden wrenched the door open, glaring from the comfort of his luxurious home. Dex shuddered a little as the warmth hit him. He was cold and so tired he was ready to drop.

"Give it to me."

Dex handed over the rolled-up wad of grubby cash, three hundred pounds in total. A decent amount, but not enough. It was never enough.

"Get inside," Braden growled. "Go clean yourself up, boy."

Dex slipped past him and made his way to the bathroom. That was the one good thing about being Braden's personal slave: the use of his bathroom. After a long night of hooking, a shower was worth far more to him than the rolled-up tenner—Dex's cut of the night—in his back pocket. Showers were like gold dust. Sometimes a good john would let him use their bathroom. One time, an oddly tactile guy had even scooped him off the bed and put him in a steaming hot bath in his grotty hotel room, but those jobs were rare. Most times, it was a quick fuck in a car or a dirty bedsit. Or worse. And for fifty quid a pop, what did you expect? Johns with real money didn't call the numbers in the back of the local rag.

Nah. The johns who called Braden's hotlines were the men too vile and seedy to find company elsewhere. The kind of men who made Dex's skin crawl. He stepped under the hot spray and shivered. *Still* made his skin crawl even hours after they'd had their hands on him.

Dex cleaned up and then lingered as long as he dared before he shut the water off and made his way like a good boy to Braden's bedroom. Any longer, and his uncle was sure to come looking for him, and Dex didn't want *that*.

He sat naked on the bed and hugged his knees to his chest. Perhaps Braden would give him some food when he was done with him. He couldn't remember the last thing he ate. It could've been the crisps he stole from a john's house a few days ago—Hula Hoops, naturally—or maybe the sausage roll Mikey had tossed his way in a rare flash of humanity.

Humanity like…. No. Dex stopped the thought in its tracks. He wouldn't think about *him*. Not now. That memory was too pure to follow him here. Too precious to share with Braden.

Braden appeared in the doorway, his hulking frame blocking the light. Dex zoned out. He'd been Braden's plaything for years, and some days, their encounters even felt normal, though a stubborn part of him knew they weren't.

Life hadn't always been this way. His childhood in Ireland had been happy and carefree, running wild with his cousins in the woodland surrounding the county they lived in. The caravans moved every year, but by and large, remained south of Kilkenny. Dex knew they were different, that they weren't accepted in the wider community, but it had never mattered.

Not until he'd turned thirteen and his father had sent him to England to earn his keep for "Uncle" Braden. In the six years since, he'd only seen his parents twice. He missed his ma, but that was life and the way of their world.

Braden cuffed his head. Dex rolled from the bed in surprise. The blow didn't hurt, but it caught him off guard. "What?"

"Don't *what* me, boy." Braden reached for a smoke, done with Dex for the night. "I said you'd better be ready when I come for you tonight. I've got a big job for you, and it starts early. Now get the fuck out and go back to whatever pit you came from."

Dex didn't need telling twice. He dressed and stepped out into the cold early morning. He picked his way across the muddy camp to the rusty caravan he called home. The yard was quiet as he walked with his head down, hands thrust in his pockets, but there were some faces around, faces he did his best to avoid.

Too bad they had other ideas.

Dex collided with a hard chest. He didn't have to look to know it belonged to Tarry, Braden's youngest son. Tarry was three years younger than Dex, but twice his size—tall, broad, and well fed. And he was a nasty, vicious twat with a penchant for making Dex's life hell.

"Watch where you're going."

Dex mumbled an apology and stepped aside, but not quick enough to avoid the swinging blow from Tarry. The force of it sent him tumbling to the ground, soaking his clothes in the wet mud.

Dazed, he lay there for a moment, absorbing the dull pain of the punch to his ribs. It had always been this way with Tarry and his brothers, and it was another reason for Dex to suspect they shared no blood... that his service to his "uncle" was a business arrangement and nothing more.

The other families on the site seemed to share Tarry and his pals' disdain for Dex, and he'd heard it said before that his own family was particularly low down in the hierarchy. For Dex, it seemed like being caught between a rock and a hard place: too far outside for any respect, but accepted enough for there to be no escape.

He pulled himself from the ground to a chorus of mocking chuckles. Ignoring them, he crawled up the steps to the freezing-cold van and tried to find the will to care what tomorrow would bring.

CHAPTER SEVEN

DEX SPENT his day cleaning caravans. The work was cold and wet, but he enjoyed it in a strange kind of way. It was a chore he'd done since he was old enough to help his da, which was as long as he could remember.

When he was done with the last van, he went to the dilapidated outbuilding that served as a stable to clean out the horse stalls. The task was his favourite job. On most sites, the animals came and went as often as the people, and some were even left behind from time to time when the caravans moved on, but not here. The site was as permanent as any Traveller camp was likely to get, and some of the horses had been there from the start.

He cleaned out the rudimentary stalls and fed each horse. When he was done, he stopped by the stalls that housed the shabbiest horses. He knew each animal by name, and he made them up for the creatures too knackered to have one. Cora, Lalla, Jon-Jo. Carric and her companion, Tauna.

Dex whistled. Tauna looked up, but Carric paid him no heed, too busy with her evening feed. He watched her with a sad smile, knowing he was the only one who bothered to feed the oldest horses, and sooner or later, he'd be forced to stop doing it too. That was the way when you lived your life at the bottom of the food chain. Once you were deemed worthless, you were left behind to die. Sometimes, he longed for that day.

It was dark when he finished his work, though he had no real idea what the time was. He said good-bye to the horses and, remembering Braden's parting shot from their early morning encounter, went to wash under the outside tap.

Mikey came to find him as he was pulling his clothes back on. "Come on, kid. Time to go."

Dex followed him to the van and stared out the window in silence as Mikey drove them to an industrial estate in the middle of town. Braden waited for them outside a nondescript building. He caught Dex's shoulder and yanked him forward, glaring at him with critical eyes. "Have you grown, boy? Maybe we need to drop you in bleach again. You sell better that way. Younger the better."

Dex kept his gaze down. He didn't remember having his hair dyed. Mikey had put something in his drink that made him sleep, and he'd woken up blond. A few weeks later, Braden had sent him to Cornwall to work on the beach. He'd wanted to cry when the last remnants of his bleached locks grew out—they were his last link to that mystical summer in Padstow.

The door to the industrial unit opened and the booted feet of another man appeared. Dex heard the murmur of voices as he bantered with Braden, but he didn't catch all the words. The English way of speaking Shelta went over his head. Besides, what did it matter? Most times, it was better not to know what he was walking into.

Mikey flicked his cheek. Dex raised his eyes and saw Braden was gone, leaving him alone with Mikey and another heavyset man.

"We'll wait outside for the boy," Mikey said. "Do what you like with him, but not his face. We make a lot of money from this pretty boy. Don't want him back as damaged goods."

The other man nodded his agreement, and Mikey disappeared into the night. The man took Dex's arm and pushed him toward the open door. "Come on, then, lad. Time to service the gorjers."

He directed Dex into the cold, drafty building and along a util-itarian corridor until they came to a locked metal door. Behind the door was a staircase that led down to some kind of cellar. Dex tensed, but his guide shoved him forward.

"Down."

Dex felt his way down the steps. He'd lost the will to be afraid years ago, but as he walked blind into a situation he knew at best would be unpleasant, his long-dormant nerves prickled to life.

The stairs seemed to go on forever, but eventually, he walked right into another solid metal door. His guide reached around him and pushed it open, shoving him forward into a warm, dim room cloaked in cigar smoke.

"Fresh meat," the man said. "We've got him all night. Who wants him first?"

Dex stared at the group of men in muted horror. He counted eight of them in total, all of varying age. The youngest was in his thirties, the oldest closer to seventy. Some of them barely glanced his way, too engrossed in the card game and whiskey set out on the table of a room that appeared to be an office, albeit with a private bar, but a few did look up, and the naked appetite in their eyes turned his stomach.

Really? A fucking orgy? It wouldn't be the first time.

One of the men stood, came over, and tipped Dex's head back with two fingers under his chin. "Looks better than the last one Braden sent. Lift your arms up, boy."

Dex obeyed, and suppressed a shiver as the man pulled his grubby sweatshirt over his head, leaving the top half of him bare. The man turned him from side to side, flicking the dark bruise formed by Tarry's fists.

Dex flinched, he couldn't help it. The man laughed and flicked him again, harder this time. "Think we might have a screamer here. Who brought a gag?"

Without warning, he yanked Dex's arms behind his back and bound them together before Dex could resist. Then he pulled a length of rope from his jacket pocket and reached for Dex's head.

Stupidly, Dex resisted and jerked away.

Irritation coloured his assailant's features. "Come 'ere, boy."

Dex clenched his fists. "Fuck off."

The man narrowed his eyes. Dex braced himself for the inevitable blow, wondering if the man would keep to the agreement and spare his face. Not that he cared. What difference did it make to him?

The punch never came. Instead, softer hands grasped his face and turned his head, and he found himself staring into the eyes of one of the younger men in the room. Clean-shaven, with scruffy, sandy brown hair, he wasn't bad-looking for a gorjer.

"Let me have a look at him before you fuck him up," the new man said.

"Squeamish, George?"

"No," George replied. "I just don't share your fetish for blood. Let me have him first, then you can do what you want."

The first man grunted and ambled back to the card game. George grasped Dex's arm and towed him from the room and back into the corridor. Once out of sight of the other men, he untied his hands.

"Don't even think of giving me lip. One move, and I'll throw you to the wolves."

That fate seemed inevitable, but Dex held his tongue and let George take him into a side room that turned out to be a fully fitted bedroom, kitted out with a huge bed and various sexual paraphernalia.

Dex eyed the whips and chains as George shut the door behind them, went to the bed, and took his watch off. George was going to fuck him, he knew that already, but how? The other men were going to break him, of that he was certain, but George seemed different. The question was, how different?

George appeared beside him. He put his hands flat on Dex's bare torso, each palm unmoving on either side of his ribcage. "You shouldn't antagonize them, you know. Do what they say, and it'll be over quicker."

Dex kept his head down, assuming a response would give George the chance to prove his point. When he didn't speak,

George sighed and began undoing his trousers. "Have it your way, kid. Don't say I didn't warn you."

He stripped Dex of his remaining clothes and pulled him over to the bed. He sat on the edge and gestured to his open jeans. "Go down on me."

Dex sank to his knees, ignoring the rough imprint of wiry carpet, and tuned out, staying aware enough only to hold steady enough not to fall flat on his face. Blowjobs were easy, painless, and quick, if he didn't feel a need to draw them out to avoid something else. He'd never understood the attraction until Seb had taken him in his mouth that night.

Seb's clean, soft bed at his back, his big, warm hands on his body, and the hot, wet heat of his mouth on his cock....

The door to the room opened and shut a few times, but Dex didn't bother to glance up. At worst, being used by Braden's clients was agonizing. One time, it had hurt so much he'd thrown up on his feet, but this... this was nothing. His mind drifted, and despite his best efforts, took him back yet again to his brief time with Seb. He wondered, as he so often did, what Seb was doing right now. Cooking, perhaps, but Dex doubted it. It was late, and it was October. Seb had often told him how quiet the shop got later in the year.

Maybe he was sleeping, or sharing his bed. Dex tried to picture him with another man, sucking him, fucking him, doing all the things they'd done together that night, but he couldn't do it, the image wouldn't come. Instead, it morphed into a bitter-sweet memory where Dex screamed in pleasure and his vision turned white.

George ruffled Dex's hair. "All done."

Dex closed his eyes, willing the image of Seb to come back. It didn't, and in the back of his mind, he was glad of it. His memories of Seb were his most precious thing. They deserved better than this. Better than *him*.

George moved away. Dex heard him getting dressed but didn't bother to move. What was the point? George was just the first of many.

He expected George to leave without a word, but he didn't. Instead, he sat on the edge of the bed and fixed Dex with a stare that made him squirm.

"I don't know what they've got in store for you, but that lot are a nasty bunch. Keep your head down and your mouth shut, got it? They'll fuck you up if you fight them and have you that way instead."

"Are you leaving?"

"Not yet. I'm going to try win my money back, but I'll get you some scotch, okay? Drink it if you can. Probably best you don't remember this."

CHAPTER EIGHT

GEORGE'S OMINOUS words proved fair warning. The bottle of scotch he slipped under the mattress helped too. Dex drank from it throughout the night, when he wasn't shackled, and by the time the sun rose, he was intoxicated enough to block out much of what happened. The whiskey didn't numb the pain, but it did help him forget to feel.

He woke in the van sometime the next day, shivering and with a vicious hacking cough from the cold. Cautiously, he crawled out of the van, but there was no one around to watch him run, naked and bloodied, across the yard to his caravan. Inside, he searched out his paltry supply of clothes, glad he'd washed them in the river a few days before. The sweatshirt was still damp, but without his coat, it would have to do.

When he was dressed, he set about completing the chores expected of him, no matter the events of the night before. He'd just finished the horses when his stomach reminded him he hadn't eaten in days. Exhausted and aching, he limped back to the caravan, weighing up the chances of Braden feeling charitable enough to pass him some food. It didn't look good. Such occasions were rare, and his other options were limited: steal some, or hunt down his own in the woods.

Stealing was tempting. He often took the blame for the

thievery of others, so why not do it anyway? At least he'd go down with a full belly. But Dex couldn't do it. Not today. He was battered enough. Briefly, he thought of the crumpled ten-pound notes buried beneath the caravan. It wasn't much, but it would buy some food, at least. Shame he wasn't allowed in the local shops.

That left hunting, but it was a day or so before Dex saw his chance. Then, under the cover of darkness, he crept into the woods, retrieved his snares from a disused badger set, and trod silently through the trees, searching for signs of rabbits or hares. On his way, he found blackberries and wild watercress, and later, a promising patch of damp moss. He dropped to his knees, crawled closer, and felt around in the dark. His hands found the rubbery, papery skin of a jackpot. Mushrooms. Some were deadly, but these were good to eat. Dex stuffed one greedily into his mouth, set a snare for a rabbit, and settled at the foot of a tree in a small clearing to wait for the rest of his dinner to make itself known. After a while, his eyes grew heavy. The dark, secluded woods were far safer than the site, and despite the cold, he soon fell asleep.

The plaintive whinny of a distressed horse woke him some-time later. Startled, he uncurled himself from his damp, uncom-fortable nest. The horses on the site weren't treated well, and he often slept with an ear open in case they needed him. He listened hard for a moment, but heard nothing more. Irritated, he shook himself. His spot in the woods was three miles from the site—too far to hear the horses there. *Maybe that john really did kick my brains in last night….*

He stretched, feeling the burning throb of bruises all over his sore body, and got to his feet. He picked his way over the ground to check his snare. He was a foot away when he heard the call of the horse again. He froze, and the hair on the back of his neck stood on end. So deep in the woods, he had to be hearing things.

He had to be.

The undergrowth rustled. A muffled shout pierced the air. Dex's heart jumped into his throat. He wasn't supposed to be out here. No one watched him to be sure he didn't leave the site, but they didn't need to. Even when he took a chance and slipped away to forage, he always went back. Where else would he go?

He swallowed a cough and backed away from the fast-approaching footsteps, knowing he should leave his snares behind and run back to the site. Whoever he could hear, he didn't want to get in their way, but the renewed, frantic cries of the distressed horse stopped him in his tracks, and indecision warred with instincts until it was too late. The first man stepped into the clearing as Dex panicked and shot up the trunk of the nearest tree.

He made it up into the leafy branches as a group of men swept flashlights and torches in a wide circle around the clearing.

Up in the tree, Dex held still and gripped the thick branch he clung to until his knuckles felt like they would surely split his skin. He counted the men. Six of them in total—two keeping watch, a leader, and two others guarding a man who appeared to be their prisoner. Dex couldn't see their faces, but deep in his hammering heart, he knew they were his own kind. Travellers were like that—invisibly and inescapably bonded.

But where was the horse? Dex scanned the clearing again, chewing his lip. The silence felt wrong, like the devil was dancing around him, and his stomach rolled when he found the outline of a dead horse, crumpled on the ground in a pool of her own blood.

Cora. Oh God. Oh God. *Cora.*

Dex didn't recognize the man held captive on the ground beside her, but, fuck, he knew the horse. The cream-coloured mare was aloof, but beneath her ingrained suspicion, she was gentle and warm. Some nights, she'd stood with her chin on his shoulder for hours, doing nothing more than simply huffing out straw-scented puffs of air. Now, in the moonlight, he could see her life-less eyes were still open, wide with shock at the violence of her death.

Dex trembled so hard he nearly fell from the branch, feeling the loss of the animal like a knife to his gut. Fear tore through his veins too. The men were from the site, they had to be, and if he was caught, there was every chance he'd share Cora's fate. Or that of the prisoner, whatever they were about to do to him. He'd heard too many stories of men disappearing in the woods, never to be seen again, to kid himself it was anything good.

The leader stepped forward, opening his arms in a deceptively friendly gesture. A familiar gesture. Dex closed his eyes as the man began to speak. He didn't have to look any closer to know he was in the presence of Uncle Braden.

There was little preamble as Braden directed his goons to hold the man against the trunk of the very tree Dex had taken shelter in. Their exchange was brief. The man shook and begged for his life, but Braden's eyes were cold and blank, and Dex wondered how many times he'd heard the same pleas.

A silence fell over the clearing. A pause. The eerie calm before a storm. Dex watched with bated breath. He wasn't ready for this... wasn't ready to watch a man die. But nothing happened, and the longer the lull went on, the more he began to hope. Perhaps he'd misjudged it, and the man had been brought here as a warning, Cora's murder an example of what would be done if the man didn't comply with whatever Braden wanted.

Then Braden put a gun to the man's head and fired.

The shot ripped through the night, bouncing off the trees and echoing louder and louder until Dex couldn't bear it. He slapped his hands over his ears. Shock rippled through him, up through his stomach and into his chest. A vicious cough jumped into his throat. He held his breath, fighting it with all he had, but it was no good. A desperate scratch of sound escaped his lungs.

He slammed his hand over his mouth, but it was too late. Braden followed the noise and looked up, and Dex knew in a heartbeat he'd been seen.

Fuck!

Dex scrambled through the branches and leaped into the air. His feet hit the ground, jarring his ankles, but he didn't look back as he ran through the woods, faster than he'd ever run before.

The trees blurred as he darted through them. Shouts echoed behind him. More gunshots pierced the air. But he didn't look back. He couldn't look back. He jumped over branches and ditches. Tripped over his own feet.

And he didn't look back.

He stumbled onto the main road, dripping with sweat, the freezing night air long forgotten. Cars and lorries honked as he dashed across the northbound carriageway, and even as he crossed into the southbound lanes, he didn't dare stop.

He reached the far side by the skin of his teeth and turned south, jogging up the hard shoulder until he reached the slip road for a service stop. It was late, but the pit stop housed an all-night café, and four or five articulated lorries lay idle in the car park, their drivers elsewhere.

Breathless, Dex crouched in a hedge and debated his options. He couldn't go back to the site. Of that he was certain. Braden would slit his throat without thinking twice. How many times had he held Dex down and uttered those very words? Question was, did it matter? Did Dex care enough to run? Maybe not, but the thought of giving Braden the satisfaction of ending his misery galled him. The bastard had taken enough.

Resolved, he considered the dormant lorries and their possible cargo. He'd hitchhiked before, but never alone, and not in England. The last time had been in Dublin when he was a boy, and his father's wise warning then echoed in his head like it had been just yesterday.

"Choose careful, lad. You don't want to sit in a truck o' pig shite all the way to Ballinasloe."

Pig shit aside, Dex was wary of the drivers. What if they checked their loads before they set off? And what if they took him right back into town? He wouldn't last a day on the streets of Hatfield. His own kind would turn him back to Braden in a heart-beat. And the gorjers? He'd only ever known one he could trust.

A broad-shouldered man with tattoos and a bandana emerged from the service station. He walked toward one of the trucks. It was the truck nearest to where Dex crouched. The shabbiest truck, the one with the flapping tarpaulin. He couldn't believe his luck. That lorry would be the easiest to get into. He had his hunting knife in his pocket. All it would take was a little cut to the already frayed securing ropes, and he could slip right in.

He tensed, ready to spring, and watched the driver carefully. If he checked his load now, chances were he'd check it again. It was a risk, a big one, but it turned out not to matter. The driver walked straight to the cab and hauled himself up into his seat without sparing a glance for his cargo.

Dex sprang from the bush and sprinted across the floodlit car park. His footsteps were deafening on the spongy, fresh tarmac, and he waited for a hand on his shoulder, a shout, anything to signal he'd been seen, but none came.

He reached the back of the lorry and ducked around the side, feeling for the loose tarpaulin. He found it, flicked open his knife, and sliced through the ropes. The whole exercise took only seconds, but to Dex, it seemed like a lifetime.

He chanced a glance over his shoulder and, seeing no one, shimmied up the side of the lorry and slipped into the drafty trailer. The lorry was full of cardboard boxes. He wove his way through them to the very middle of the trailer. Once there, he stopped and counted the frantic beat of his heart until it slowed to a dull roar. There was no sound from the outside. He'd made it. He was safe, for now, at least.

Exhausted, he hunkered down behind a giant cardboard box. Blood on his shoes caught his eye, and though he knew it wasn't hers, he thought of Cora lying dead in the woods. Thought of the horses he'd left behind. Tauna, Carric, and their stable mates. Without him, most of them would surely starve.

The gravity of what he'd done hit him like a kick to the chest. He shook and tears streamed in hot tracks down his face. The lorry rumbled to life, and only his fist in his mouth muffled his scream.

CHAPTER NINE

THE LORRY stopped around dawn. The driver got out, but Dex stayed huddled in the back, holding his breath and wound so tight every nerve in his body felt like it would snap, until he felt safe enough to shuffle to the side of the trailer.

Cautiously, he peered through the tarpaulin and scanned the car park. There didn't seem to be anyone around, so he took a chance, slithered out of the trailer, and crept around the cab of the lorry. He hadn't heard the driver lock up, and sure enough, when he tried the door, it opened right up. After another furtive glance around, he swiped a jacket, a can of Coke, and a wallet from the passenger seat.

There wasn't much in the wallet—twenty quid—but it served its purpose. He used it to pay a foreign truck driver to buy him a sandwich and take him the rest of the way to London. The Polish driver didn't speak much English, but when he let Dex out of the cab in the capital, he told him he was in Regent's Park.

Dex watched the lorry disappear into the heavy traffic, and then, lacking any better ideas, he shoved his hands in his pockets and started walking. He walked all day, and by nightfall, he found himself in a busy shopping district bustling with commuters and tourists. Alarmed, he trailed to a stop. He'd never seen such crowded streets. Living out on the site, he didn't mix much with the outside world, at least not like this. People jostled and shoved him, taking no notice of him at all. Instinctively, he shrank back, edging away from the pavement until he found the blocked-up entrance of a disused alleyway.

He crouched down, hugging his knees to his chest. His heart pounded. He'd escaped, he was free. But what the fuck did he do now? He had no money, no food, and no place to sleep.

Not even a rusty bloody caravan.

Despair swept over him. He pushed his face into his knees and wrapped his arms over his head. He'd run for his life, only to confirm what he already knew: there was nothing else out there.

Not for him.

DEX SPENT the night huddled behind a rubbish skip, and the pattern continued in the week or so that followed. By day, he walked the streets with no care of where he was going, and when night fell, he followed the lead of the other vagrants and lay down in the shiny shop doorways, absorbing the heat from the steam grates.

Eventually his aimless wandering took him away from the affluent shopping and tourist district and in the direction the stars told him was northeast.

From time to time, he managed to steal food from the market stalls, but most days, he went hungry, so hungry he felt like his stomach was trying to eat itself. Hunger was a way of life for him, but this was different. Before, he'd had things to distract him. Chores. Hooking. Violence. A world of fear, but alone on the streets now, all he felt was the destructive pain of his empty belly.

When the weather turned too wet to sleep outside, Dex took shelter in the Underground stations, particularly the tunnels that took commuters to the escalators that led belowground. The tunnels were light and warm, and the station security guards didn't venture far from the platforms.

One night he sat, half-dozing, with his back to the wall and his head in his hands. People passed him by. Some even left handfuls of pocket change at his feet, but he didn't look up until a man nudged him with his foot.

"Working boy? How much?"

Dex blinked under the harsh fluorescent lights of the tunnel. It took a moment to comprehend what the man meant. Then it was all too easy to nod and follow the man into the public toilets. At this time of night, they were deserted, and Dex found himself alone with the man.

"How much for head?"

"Thirty."

The man shook his head. "For that much, I fuck you. I have protection."

Dex thought quickly. He'd never negotiated a price for himself before. "Forty for both."

"Done."

It didn't take long, less than ten minutes, and the man wasn't the last to sense Dex could be more than a simple beggar. Dex turned two more tricks that night, and more in the days that followed before the police finally moved him on.

He tried again at the next station, but this time, he picked up a bad john, the kind of john who got off on blood and pain. The john slammed him face-first into a tiled wall and wrapped his hand around his throat, choking him until he passed out. He woke up on the filthy toilet floor, bleeding and with every crumpled note he'd earned robbed from the back pocket of his tatty jeans.

He gave up hooking after that. The experience was nothing he hadn't been through before, but without Mikey and Braden scooping him up and shoving him back out there, he lost his nerve. He left the area and moved on, his head clearer than it had been since he'd escaped the woods of Hertfordshire. It had felt normal to turn a few tricks, for a while, at least. Reminded him who he was. What he deserved. And when the change in his pocket finally ran out, the hunger in his belly became easier to bear.

He'd been in London a month when he drifted into a borough a fellow tramp told him was Stoke Newington. The borough was brightly coloured and bohemian, with a heady sense of danger. Though Dex lived in the shadows, snatching sleep by day and lurking at night, he felt oddly at home.

To survive, he returned to his roots, to foraging, but this time, the urban kind, skulking in alleyways and restaurant bin yards. He was passing aimlessly through a dimly lit backstreet one night when his daze was broken by the sight of a man not much older than him being slung onto the pavement from the open back doors of a restaurant kitchen.

Startled, Dex took a step back, flattening himself against a wall. The man on the ground scrambled to his feet as his assailant burst out on to the street.

"Bugger off," the new man on the scene growled. "Thieving arsehole. Get the fuck out of here before I kick some decency into you."

From his place in the shadows, Dex watched the thief slink away. The scent of cigarette smoke reached his nose, telling him the second man had sat down on the back steps and lit a fag, leaving him two choices: stay right where he was until the man went inside, or step out of the shadows and slip past in the hope the man wouldn't see where he'd come from.

The rumble of thunder made up his mind. Getting his clothes wet was a pain in the arse. He'd take suspicion and a few harsh words over that any day.

He hoped to pass right by the man unseen, but, of course, nothing was ever that easy. The man called out as soon as he saw him.

"Hey, kid. You looking for work?"

Dex glanced behind him, unsure if the civil question was meant for him. "Um, pardon?"

His voice was scratchy and hoarse. It was the first time he'd spoken in days, and he still had the cough he'd picked up from his night spent naked in the back of Mikey's van.

The man appraised him through a cloud of smoke. "You look

like you need a job, and I'm down a pot washer. Interested? It's hard bloody work, but I'll pay you."

Dumbly, Dex nodded. He'd never had a real job before, but he knew hard work, and he knew how to wash a pot.

"How old are you?"

"Nineteen."

"Sure about that? Don't want the council giving me grief."

"I'm sure," Dex hedged. For once, he was telling the truth, but he had no way of proving it. He'd never had the documents that proved who he was, how old he was, and where he came from. Braden had all that, if they'd ever existed at all.

It seemed an age before the man flicked his cigarette into the gutter and got to his feet. "Come on, then."

Dex followed him into the kitchen. A wall of heat hit him. A thick wave of air, heavy with the scent of cooking food. Steaming pots on the stove. Meat on the flaming chargrill. He was sure he could even see chips in the fryer. A painful growl of hunger gripped his gut. He stumbled but kept walking, all the way through the kitchen until they came to a small, carpeted staircase.

The man stopped and gestured for him to go ahead. Dex hesitated. How many times had he preceded Braden or Mikey like a lamb to the slaughter?

"You're going to need some whites," the man said.

Dex stared at him, trying to read his slightly bored expression. The man was big and heavyset, with a beer belly hanging over his checked trousers. His face was young, but his gut gave him away as being at least thirty years older than Dex.

The man sighed. "Suit yerself. I'll bring 'em down. You can change in the bogs. Wait here."

Dex waited, and the man soon reappeared with a pair of patterned trousers, a white T-Shirt, and a short-sleeved white jacket that looked *huge*. With his other hand, the man offered him a pair of black rubber shoes.

"Crocs," he said. "Stop you slipping by the dishwasher."

Dex took the pile of clothes and changed in the small cloak-room by the kitchen. The jacket and trousers were far too big for him, and the man—*Rick*—let out a deep guffaw when he emerged.

"Bloody hell. You look like a refugee. Come here."

Dex stood awkward and tense as Rick rolled his sleeves up and folded the waistband of his trousers down over a rudimentary belt made from knotted cling film, and then he followed him back through the kitchen area to a sink full of dirty pots and pans.

"Get through that lot before service ends, and you've got yourself a gig."

Rick said it like a challenge, but Dex knew it wouldn't take long to wash up the pans. Some of them had burned-on grease, but with plenty of hot water at his disposal, it would come away easily enough.

He got started, and as the evening progressed, he kept his head down and cleaned anything that came his way. At some point, a chef brought him a cup of coffee and a bowl of chips, and later, when all the work was done for the night, Rick reappeared with his clothes. Clothes that looked and smelled suspiciously clean.

"There's a machine and a dryer upstairs, lad. The missus was washing the lunchtime linens anyway."

Dex took his clothes and wrapped his arms around them. They were all he had in the world, and he didn't know whether to be grateful or annoyed. Or bloody embarrassed. "Thanks."

"What's your name?"

"Dex."

"Here you go, Dex." Rick slapped a twenty-pound note in his hand. "Good work today. Come back tomorrow at 3:00 p.m. Show up clean, on time, and ready to work, and I'll start paying you properly."

CHAPTER TEN

DEX SHOWED up the next day, and the day after that, and the day after that. Before he knew it, a week had gone by and he had a job. A real job that, barring his brief stint as a solo hooker, paid more money than he'd ever had in his life. Thirty quid a day meant food and clothes, and with Rick's help, a sparsely furnished room at a hostel down the road.

The hostel was noisy and scary, but exhausted by long shifts in the restaurant kitchen and guarded by a lock on the door, Dex found he could sleep away most of his time there, curled up on the bare mattress in the corner. He used the shower at the restaurant, washed his clothes at the restaurant, and ate most of his meals there too. The hostel was nothing more than a bolt-hole away from the streets.

One morning, he started his shift early. Rick was hosting a big lunchtime event, and he'd called everyone in to help get ready.

"All hands on deck, kid," he'd said.

Dex left the hostel at dawn and sloped along the deserted streets, his only company the bin men throwing wheelie bins at the slow-moving rubbish truck. He walked with his head down and his hands in his pockets. A fight in the hostel corridors had woken him in the night, and he was tired and distracted.

A loud shout made him jump. He stumbled, tripped over his

own feet, and whirled around. Behind him, he saw the bin men and a small group of teenagers who appeared to be setting up a market stall. He let out the breath caught in his chest. It was okay. It wasn't *them*. He was still safe.

Yeah, but for how long?

The voice in Dex's head taunted him the rest of the way to the restaurant. Staying in one place was stupid. It was safer to keep moving, keep running, and hope his old life never caught up with him. Trouble was, he couldn't find the will to leave the safe haven he'd found in Stoke Newington, no matter how great the risk. And it was a big risk. Braden wouldn't come after him to silence him. Travellers didn't talk to the police—or anyone else—about their own business. No. Braden would hunt him down to take him back. To reclaim what was his.

"You're mine now, boy. You belong to me."

Dex's escape would be seen as an insult... an embarrassment, and if Braden caught up with him, there was no doubt he wouldn't be kind enough to kill him.

So why not keep moving? Hide himself away? Perhaps he didn't care enough to bother, or maybe, just maybe, he was tired of running.

Dex continued on his way.

At the restaurant, he was the first back-of-house employee to arrive. Bernie, Rick's wife, let him in and gave him a cup of tea while he set to work turning the dishwasher on and cleaning the last few dishes left by lingering wait staff the night before.

A delivery arrived at the back door as he was finishing up. Rick was nowhere to be seen, so Dex fetched Bernie to deal with the grumpy driver. After, he helped her carry the boxes in. He didn't pay much attention to the contents—his place was by the dishwasher. Bernie's horrified screech caught him off guard.

For the second time that day, his stomach jumped into his throat. "What's wrong?"

Bernie slapped her hand over her mouth and pointed to the box she'd dropped on the counter belonging to the starter chef.

Dex followed her gaze to the box, but it contained nothing but six braced pairs of rabbits. "You didn't want the rabbits?"

Bernie removed her hand and cringed. "Not bloody whole ones. Jesus, Mary, and Joseph. Go and get the order pad."

Dex fetched the pad and held it out, but Bernie was talking on the phone. She put her hand over the mouthpiece. "Check the order sheet, duck. See what it says. This idiot is sure we ordered them whole."

Dex stared mutely at the order pad, counted to ten, and held it out again. "I can't see them."

Irritated, Bernie snatched the pad and glared at it. When she found what she was looking for, she cursed and hung up the phone. "Bollocks," she said again. "Rick's going to kill me. I ordered the wrong ones."

Dex peeked into the box again. The rabbits were wild, strong boned, and supple. And fresh too. He could tell they'd only been shot the night before. "What's wrong with them?"

"They usually come in jointed. Rick's going to go spare when he sees them. I'll have to go out and get some more."

"Can't you cut them up?"

Bernie shook her head, already flapping and looking for her keys. "He's at the fish market. He won't have time to cook the dish if he has to joint them too, and the others aren't in till ten."

"I can cut them."

Bernie paused and gave him a strange look. "Really? You know how to do that?"

Dex nodded and pulled the box closer. He knew his way round a dead rabbit. Hares and squirrels too. "Which board do I use?"

"Red for raw meat. Hang on. I'll get you a knife. Are you sure you've done this before?"

"A few times. How do you want them?"

Bernie shrugged. "Jointed, and I suppose that means skinned too."

"Unless you want to eat the fur."

Bernie pulled a face. "Christ, no. I can't imagine why anyone would want to eat a rabbit, anyway." She pulled the first rabbit from the box and laid it on the board with a shudder. "How about we try with one, and if it doesn't work out, we can hide the evidence and I'll face the music."

Dex reached for the rabbit and set to work, skinning it and removing the head before he cut off the legs. Left with the saddle, he separated the ribs and trimmed off the excess sinew. The familiar exercise took a few minutes, and when he was done, he looked up to find Bernie watching him with shrewd eyes.

"You really have done that before, eh?"

"My da taught me."

Bernie peered over his shoulder at the jointed rabbit. "Looks to me like he taught you well. Think you can finish the box before Rick gets back from the fish yard?"

"How long will he be?"

"Twenty minutes?"

Dex counted the eleven remaining rabbits and shrugged. "I can try."

And try he did. By the time Rick appeared in the kitchen half an hour later, the only evidence of Rabbitgate was the crumbs of the bacon sandwich Bernie had brought him in gratitude.

The rest of the day passed in a steamy haze of dirty dishes, pots, and pans. No one mentioned the rabbits, and as was his habit, Dex kept his head down and worked hard. There were six chefs on Rick's team who worked on varying shift patterns. They all seemed nice enough, but he knew better than to look them in the eye.

After the busy dinner service, he found himself the last one left in the kitchen. He swept and mopped the floors, and then turned out the lights before heading upstairs to get changed.

"Not so fast."

Dex jumped a mile, one foot frozen on the stairs. He turned to face Rick with a deep sense of foreboding. Rick had been in and out of the kitchen all day, working the bar and generally doing anything that needed doing, but he'd disappeared into the office a while ago. Perhaps he'd read the order pad.

Rick beckoned him down from the stairs. "Come with me."

Dex followed him with trepidation, knowing better than to argue. If Rick was angry, Dex would accept his punishment. It was easier that way. He followed Rick to the food prep area of the kitchen, and waited, as instructed, as Rick vanished into the huge walk-in fridge.

Rick returned with a large white tray of various items of meat and fish. "Get some boards and some knives. Red for the meat, yellow for poultry, and blue for the fish."

Dex coughed into his elbow and obeyed, mystified. What was Rick going to do? Make him eat raw chicken or something? Teach him a lesson?

He set out the boards and filled a tub with warm water for the knives. Rick stepped back and folded his arms across his chest. "Get the pheasants and cut them into quarters for me."

Dex found the brace of birds and made short work of cutting them up. Rick inspected his work, but Dex didn't dare try to read his expression.

"Now the lamb," Rick said. "Get the ribs off and portion the racks."

Dex reached for the sheep carcass and frowned. He'd never seen one before, but it looked pretty similar to a goat. He picked out a slightly bigger knife and set to work. It didn't take long, and when he was done, Rick seemed amused.

"Now the fish. Fillet them."

"Take the bones out?"

"That's right."

Dex moved to the blue board, changed his knife, and removed the flesh from the three fish Rick set out in front of him. He stood back when he was finished and chewed on his lip. It had been a while since he'd tackled a fish. There was no real water near the site in Hatfield, only the stream that grew the wild watercress.

Rick laughed. The chuckle came from deep in his belly, and for the umpteenth time that day, Dex jumped out of his skin.

"Easy now." Rick dropped a heavy hand on his shoulder. "Was

just testing Bernie's loose tongue. You've got some skills there, lad. You ever worked in a kitchen before?"

Dex coughed into his elbow again. "No."

"Didn't think so. You butcher like the best poacher I've ever seen. Don't tell me I'm right. I don't want to know."

Dex followed his advice and took the used boards and equipment to the sink. The dishwasher was drained and off for the day, but he knew Rick didn't like dirty things left overnight. He didn't realise Rick had followed him until he sensed his presence, leaning on the wall by the plate racks.

"How would you feel about starting your shifts a little earlier, say, around ten, rather than twelve?"

Dex shrugged. It made no difference to him. It wasn't like he had anything else to do, and the less time he spent in the hostel, the better.

Rick took his silence as agreement. "Good lad. Be here at ten tomorrow. Got somewhere to take you."

Dex duly turned up on time the following morning to discover Rick had decided to take him to a walk-in centre attached to Homerton Hospital.

"You need to see a quack about that cough," he said in a tone that left no room for argument. "The missus thinks you've got TB. Can't have that if you're going to be touching the food proper."

"TB? Like a badger?" Dex eyed the waiting room warily. He'd never seen a real doctor before. Only mad Aunt Madge with her herbs back in Ireland, and that had been more than a decade ago.

"If you say so." Rick pointed to a chair in the corner. "Sit down. I'll get you signed in."

Dex didn't have the balls to point out he couldn't sign him in without knowing his full name, but it turned out not to matter. Rick had brought him to an open clinic for illegal immigrants, and no one asked him any questions at all.

And he didn't have TB or any other infectious diseases they'd tested his blood for. Just bronchitis, apparently, and he was given a bottle of big white pills to take every day for the next two weeks.

He found Rick on the phone when he emerged from the clinic. Dex waited beside him until he hung up the phone with a heavy sigh.

"Looks like I found your hidden talents just in time. Iggy's walked out on us. He's gone back to bloody Bristol to make up with that slag he was shagging last year."

Dex nodded like he had a clue what Rick was talking about. He didn't. He knew who Iggy was, of course, but he had no idea who he'd been fucking. "Is he coming back?"

"Nope. Doesn't look like it. What do you say, kid? Want to help me out and learn to cook?"

CHAPTER ELEVEN

THE BIG white pills gave Dex a headache and left him lethargic and dopey. He preferred the cough, but with Bernie on his case, he toed the line and dutifully took the pills, and he spent the next few weeks learning the ropes of food preparation and supporting the chefs in the kitchen during service.

He peeled potatoes and cut up meat for the mainline chefs, prepared garnishes and salads for the starter chefs, and chopped more onions than he'd ever seen in his life. By and large, he enjoyed the work, and it made a change from washing pots.

Saturday nights were the busiest. And the most stressful. He kept his head down and his opinions to himself, but it didn't take long to figure out the kitchen was a pressure cooker when service didn't go according to plan.

One evening, he knew as soon as the first order came in it was going to be one of *those* nights. The chaos began when a steak came back. Rick, who was running Iggy's abandoned dessert section, was furious. Steaks were expensive, and seeing one end up in the bin put him in a bad mood for the rest of service.

"Dex! Get me another two tubs of ice cream. There's no prep on this fucking station."

Dex fetched the ice cream tubs and put them in the small freezer on the dessert section. Rick looked at the tubs and shook his head. "Goddamn bought-in crap. We used to make our own, but who's got the time for that when no twat wants to hold down a job?"

The question seemed rhetorical. Dex kept his gaze on the task at hand, rearranging the freezer shelves to accommodate the ice cream, but Rick got impatient. He reached over Dex's head, jammed the tubs in at an awkward angle, and kicked the door shut with a grunt.

The door slammed with a sickening thud. Rick stomped away like nothing had happened, but for Dex it felt like the world had imploded....

"Told you he looked better blond. Get him on the table. Put the cuffs on. Yeah, that's right. Don't worry, he's not a screamer. He'll be good here until we get back. Lock that door behind you."

Another loud slam brought Dex back to the present. Rick dropped a white chopping board down on the counter. "Get off the floor, Dex. I don't pay you to sit around."

Dex scrambled to his feet and slunk to the dishwasher. His head was spinning like he hadn't eaten in days. Come to think of it, he'd forgotten to eat the fried egg bap someone had passed him that morning, distracted by the huge pile of weird little birds Rick had asked him to butcher. Quail, apparently. They had the same anatomy as a chicken, but they looked like spindly aliens.

Being invisible was an art he'd practiced most of his life. He stuck close to the pot wash area for the rest of the night, trying to avoid the deteriorating atmosphere in the kitchen, and he'd have climbed right into the dishwasher itself if it meant avoiding confrontation.

But even hidden by the crockery stands and towering plate racks, he couldn't escape the worsening wrath of Rick and the other chefs. He knew their aggression wasn't personal, but he buckled under the weight of it, lost his focus, dropped things, and drew attention to himself—a grave error where he came from, and a big mistake during a dinner service that was fast becoming a war zone.

Chefs shouted. Waitresses cried. Even Bernie came in from the bar and got involved, until eventually Rick snapped and hurled a metal spatula across the kitchen.

There were several people between Dex and missile, and he would never be sure Rick even meant to hit him. But it did hit him. It sliced into his temple in a bruising blow and knocked him off balance.

Dex blinked, more surprised than anything. Rick's temper had been boiling over all night, but getting whacked with a spatula caught Dex off guard.

And scared the shit out of him. The kitchen became a dark, deserted alleyway, his face mashed into a brick wall. A cramped, grubby car with a sweaty, heaving body behind him. Chained to the bed in Uncle Braden's mobile home....

Bernie stepped in front of him, her expression one of fury. He flinched and stepped back, but she persisted and caught his arm, and he realised her anger wasn't aimed at him. "Come on, sweetie. Let's go outside."

No one looked their way as Dex let Bernie lead him out to the frost-covered bin yard. Service went on despite the violent disruption, and were it not for the sharp pain in the side of his already aching head, he'd have thought he'd imagined the whole incident.

He shrugged out of Bernie's grasp and walked out into the night. The air was cold and the sky was clear. He stared up at the stars, wondering if his ma's bedtime tales of long-dead gypsies haunting the skies were really true. Maybe his nan was up there somewhere. If he closed his eyes and thought about it really hard, he could just about recall her pinched face and bony fingers.

"Here, put some ice on that shiner," Bernie said. "You're going to feel that tomorrow."

Dex took the ice-filled cloth Bernie passed him, but didn't press it to the throbbing bruise on his head. Couldn't see how it would help.

Bernie took advantage of his silence and stepped closer, rubbing his shoulder. "What's the matter, sweetie? You're not yourself. Do you still feel poorly?"

Dex rolled his eyes. Rick, Bernie, and his coworkers were constantly on his case for being too quiet. "I'm okay."

Bernie eyed him, unconvinced. "Go home, Dex. Get some sleep. You work every day. It's about time you took an early finish."

Dex snapped his gaze to her, alarmed. "I've still got stuff to do. Rick—"

"*Rick* will answer to me when this bloody service finally ends. Don't worry about him, sweetheart. It's just one of those days, and you got caught in the wrong place at the wrong time. This *isn't* your fault."

Rick had proved himself a formidable foe tonight, but he had nothing on Bernie. She was a towering force of Liverpudlian menace, and wasn't taking no for an answer.

Dex slipped upstairs, got changed, and left the restaurant without encountering another soul. He walked home in a daze. He hadn't felt right since he'd woken that morning, and the disastrous shift at the restaurant topped off a bad day all round. All he wanted was to curl up on his bare mattress and forget it'd ever happened. Or maybe forget he existed at all. It had to be a sign… an omen of some kind. He'd known from the start he was living on borrowed time, and perhaps that time had come to an end.

He collided face-first with something warm and hard… warm, hard, and stinking of hay.

"Oi! Watch where you're going."

Dex stumbled back. The voice came from somewhere above him, and he looked up to see he'd walked straight into the side of a patrolling police horse. He felt his eyes widen. He'd spent his life around horses, but he'd never seen an animal as huge as the sleek black stallion.

The policeman glared down at him. "Move it along. If you're drunk, go home."

The horse walked on, ambling at a sedate pace that gave him an almost regal air. Dex stared after him, taking in the animal's thick, corded muscles and gleaming coat. It was the healthiest horse he'd ever seen. Carric and Tauna flashed into his mind.

Carric was lame, and Tauna had been so hungry last time he'd fed them, she'd eaten half of Carric's feed before Carric could get to it. There hadn't been enough to give Carric any more grain, and he'd fallen asleep that night to the mournful call of the starving mare.

Until Mikey had come to get him.

Dex let himself into the hostel and made his way to his room, sticking close to the walls and avoiding eye contact with the other residents. His head hurt, and he felt unsettled and sick. He thought he'd feel better when he locked his door behind him, but it wasn't to be. He stumbled to his mattress in the corner and lay down, feeling like his spinning head would topple him right off the earth. Sleep found him, but his dreams were plagued by the cries of the horses he'd left behind in Hatfield. Cora came to him too, her lifeless face reanimating to become frantic and desperate, calling to him for help. But he didn't dream of the man bound at the foot of the tree with a gun to his head. He never had, and in the rare moments he ever thought of him, he knew he wouldn't.

In the morning, Dex woke drenched in sweat. His stomach roiled until he leaned over the side of the mattress and threw up. Panting, he slapped a shaky hand over his mouth. He felt awful, like he'd been tipped upside down and shaken until his insides came out, but as his stomach heaved to empty itself of its phantom contents, he felt like a weight was floating away from his body. By the time he'd cleaned up the mess and got ready for work, he felt a lot better.

He was an hour early for his shift, but Rick was waiting for him on the back steps, blowing smoke from his ever-present cigarette into the early morning sky.

Rick put two fingers under Dex's chin, tilting his face so he could see it better. He winced when he saw the jagged red line on his temple, surrounded by a faint, murky bruise. "Sorry, kid. Things got a little lairy last night, eh?"

Dex said nothing, forcing himself not to squirm under Rick's light touch. What was there to say? Bernie said he'd been in the wrong place at the wrong time, but he'd yet to find that magical place where no one felt the need to take a swing at him.

Rick gave him a long look and sighed. "Bernie ripped me a new one last night, just so you know. Can't promise I won't chew you out again—it's how kitchens work—but I'll try and keep my utensils to myself next time. Deal?"

"Works for me."

"All right, lad." Rick grinned and lit another cigarette. "Go get cleaned up and ready for lunch. I'll get the missus to bring you a butty."

It was the first and only time the incident was ever mentioned. Bernie's prophecy that the storm would pass turned out to be true, and a week or so later, with his head fully healed, Dex all but forgot it too.

One night in early December, he finished mopping the kitchen around midnight. He was about to leave when Rick called him into the bar.

"Hey, kid. Come and have a drink with us. We're celebrating."

Dex accepted a pint of cold lager. He didn't often stay after his shifts, preferring to keep to himself, but occasionally, Rick wouldn't let him escape. "What are you celebrating?"

"A fucking miracle, that's what. We've got a new dessert chef. Starts in the morning. Can hardly believe it. Never thought we'd get someone this close to Christmas. He's good too. I worked with him in Piccadilly before he buggered off down south."

Dex absorbed the information with muted interest. Chefs seem to come and go every week, but he knew Rick had been struggling trying to manage the dessert section by himself. He nodded his good wishes, finished his beer, and headed home without giving it much more thought.

He was first in the kitchen the next morning, and he set to work getting ready for the day... until he got the distinct impression he wasn't alone. A muffled curse sounded from the back of the kitchen. Curious, Dex took the biggest pan and carried it over to the stove to get a better look at who was poking about in the dessert fridge.

A strong, muscular back greeted him. Dex froze, though he

didn't know why, and perhaps sensing a presence behind him, the owner of the back turned and looked over his shoulder.

The world stopped spinning. Dex's heart stalled, and his blood began to rush so fast he felt he would surely faint. The broad-shouldered man had shorter hair than he remembered, and he looked as stunned as Dex felt, but his hypnotic blue gaze was just the same.

Dex made a sound, a strangled sound distorted by the breath caught in his throat. He dropped the heavy pan to the floor. No. It couldn't be. The stranger was the man of his dreams, and not a stranger at all.

The stranger was the man Dex wanted to hold him forever.

CHAPTER TWELVE

THE PAN hit the tiled floor with a deafening clatter. Cold water sloshed over Dex's feet. Shaken, he dropped to his knees to clear it up, his heart hammering. He was vaguely aware of the stranger... of *Seb*... getting to his feet, but he didn't dare look up. *Couldn't* look up. He was imagining things. Had to be. Seb lived in Padstow, and by his thick, Cornish accent, he'd lived there all his life. He wasn't supposed to be here. What the fuck was he doing in London? Doing *here*, of all fucking places.

"Dex."

It wasn't a question. Seb's voice was steady and sure, and sounded the same as it had eighteen months ago when they'd shared a bed... shared kisses, body heat, and so much more. Dex stared at the water pooling around his feet. Watched it spread like oozing blood under the upright refrigerator. The fridge held all the prep for the main line section, prep he was supposed to be replenishing. Rick....

"*Dex.*"

No.

Dex sucked in a breath and got to his feet, reaching for the paper towel dispenser on the wall. When he'd realised that, even away from Braden's control, he'd never be safe enough to risk returning to Padstow, he'd locked Seb in a box at the very bottom of his heart, never daring to dream he'd ever see him again. And now, just the sound of his voice hurt, cutting deep into a wound barely healed.

No. Dex closed his eyes. He couldn't do this. Not now. Maybe not ever.

Rick stomped into the kitchen. He retrieved the pan and slung it on the stove without seeming to care how it had found its way to the floor. "Clean that water up, Dex. Don't fancy falling on my arse before lunch. Have you met Seb?"

Dex nodded slowly. "Just now."

Seb's eyes darkened. It was subtle, and perhaps no one else would've noticed, but to Dex, it was like a wave swirling up from the sea on a black, stormy night. He ducked his head and set about blotting the spilled water from the floor. Seb was angry, he could tell, but what was he supposed to say? *"It's okay. I know him. I know he has a freckle behind his ear and a tiny scar on his belly. I know him, because I promised him I'd never forget him."*

He didn't say it, and neither did Seb. Seb didn't say anything at all. His expression was darkly inscrutable, and unable to take the awkward silence, Dex fled the dessert counter and returned to his place by the pot wash.

Seb's melodic voice taunted him for the rest of the morning— calling out to the other chefs, most of whom seemed to already know him. Introducing himself to the front-of-house staff, bantering with Rick. It was wonderful and horrible. Comforting and utterly disturbing. He felt like he'd been dropped in another world. He'd never shared Seb with anyone, and he didn't recognize this jovial, sociable side of him. Every moment they'd spent together had been theirs alone.

And why do you think that was? Do you think he wanted people knowing he had a dirty pikey in his shop?

Dex's hands shook. He'd been called a dirty pikey his whole life, but the thought of the words falling from Seb's mouth made him feel cold all over.

Around noon, Rick approached Dex and dropped a heavy hand on his shoulder. "I'm heading out to meet a supplier. Want to keep me company?"

Dex set down his knife with more care than he really wanted to. The thought of climbing into Rick's sleek BMW was terrifying, but his mind was racing so fast it hurt, and the desire to escape the heavy air of the kitchen, if only for a few hours, was too tempting to pass up.

He'd never sat in the front seat of a car before. The sleek leather seats enveloped him like a cocoon, a very warm cocoon when Rick turned the heat on. The car was a far cry from being thrown around in the back of a rusty van, and despite the turmoil in his heart, or maybe because of it, he fell asleep.

Rick woke him when they reached a place called Walthamstow and pointed to a small warehouse. "Abattoir," he said. "Jones slaughters all his own meat. Best butcher in London. Come on, I'll show you."

He led Dex to the back of the building and introduced him to Jones, a butcher with the broadest Scottish accent he'd ever heard. Jones was pleasant enough, but the sight of row upon row of knives and cleavers lined up on the walls and the smell of fresh blood made Dex nervous. He stood in the corner with his back to the wall, chewing on his lip, until Rick called him forward.

"Look at this." He gestured to a whole pig Jones had laid out on the huge wooden table. "Gloucester Old Spot. See this fat here? It's the best bit."

Dex nodded, silent and dumb. Rick was always saying shit like that, like Dex had a clue what he was talking about. "Are you taking this back to the restaurant?" he finally asked.

"When Jones has cut it up for me. Come stand here and watch. I reckon you'll pick it up pretty quick."

Rick wasn't wrong. Dex watched Jones work his butchering tools efficiently through one half of the pig, and it wasn't hard to follow the natural lines of the body. The cuts were a little different from those of the meats he already knew, but he thought he could figure it out. The other thing he liked was that no cut of the pig went to waste. Each part was neatly packed and labelled.

"Want a go?" Jones held out the long butchering knife.

Dex glanced at Rick.

Rick shrugged and nudged him forward. "Go on. You've got a good eye. I think I can trust you with three hundred quid's worth of meat."

Dex wasn't so sure, but he took the knife anyway, and a little while later, was pleasantly surprised to see the clean piles of meat set out in front of him. Butchery wasn't a skill that interested him, but Rick seemed pleased every time he did it, and that was good enough for him. Life was far easier if you did things to make your master smile.

Dex managed to stay awake on the journey back to the restaurant. He watched the city fly by with muted interest, barely noticing the bustle until something caught his eye. He pointed at the neon-pink sign and frowned. "I keep seeing that everywhere. What is it?"

Rick shot him a strange look. "It's the Olympics, kid. London 2012?" Dex was mystified, and his confusion in turn seemed to mystify Rick. "Where the hell were you all summer? Under a bloody rock?"

Dex didn't have an answer for that, and went back to staring out the window. His mind drifted to Seb as they neared the restaurant. He felt tense and on edge, like a bomb was about to fall from the sky and obliterate Seb from his life again, like the morning had been a dream and he'd never been there at all.

The notion made his chest ache. He'd left Seb behind in Padstow, and it had hurt so much he could hardly breathe. Still hurt, even now. He thought back to those hazy summer months more than a year ago. Thought of the first time he'd seen Seb's magical blue eyes in the crazy mess of his fudge shop kitchen. Thought of that mind-blowing moment when he'd felt Seb's lips on his neck.

He wondered if Seb would ever know he was the only man he'd ever *chosen* to fuck him.

Seb looked up as they came in. He was once again the only one in the kitchen, and something was off. Something had changed. It took Dex a moment to realise he'd moved the whole dessert section around in their absence.

"Where'd you go? Anywhere fun?"

Seb directed his question at Dex, but Rick answered for him. "Walthamstow. Had to see a man about a beast. You should see this one with a whole pig." He cuffed Dex's shoulder. "Quite a butcher under all that hair."

Seb paused in whatever he was doing on the pudding counter, his gaze curious and almost amused. "Where did you learn that, Dex?"

There was no escape this time, and Dex resisted a strange urge to hide behind Rick. "My da."

Seb stared at him, waiting for him to elaborate, but Dex lost his nerve and fled the kitchen to get changed before any more questions came his way.

There were more chefs in the kitchen by the time he got back, and Seb was still busy putting the dessert section back together ready for the evening rush. He didn't glance up as Dex drifted past him, and for a precious few hours, Dex was almost able to convince himself he wasn't there at all.

He put his head down and got on with his jobs, trying to ignore the conflicting emotions gnawing at his belly. Trying to ignore the tingling presence of the man he'd tried so hard to forget. He'd always felt safe with Seb, like his broad shoulders and big hands could protect him from anything, but he felt unsettled now, clumsy and stupid, and it didn't help that nothing in the back area of the kitchen was where it should've been. It seemed Seb had disrupted more than Dex's dormant heart.

It was just before six when Rick came looking for him again. "Good news, lad," he said without waiting for Dex to follow him out of the kitchen. "You're officially promoted. New pot washer starts tonight."

Dex stopped on his way to the kitchen door. "Promoted? To what?"

"That's up to you. I want you to do a bit more cooking, but you need to figure out which section suits you best. Spend some time on all of them. In fact, why don't you start on puds with Seb? He can probably use a hand while he gets settled in."

"What?"

"Seb," Rick repeated with surprising patience. "Go and help him, learn from him, and next week, you can try something else."

Dex didn't move until Rick grasped his shoulders and literally pushed him across the kitchen. He stumbled into the dessert section, off-balance from Rick's playful shove, and narrowly missed colliding with Seb. Seb reached out to steady him, but Dex sidestepped his hand and wound up by the wall, his eyes fixed on the floor.

Seb sighed. "You want to help me make brownies?"

With Rick's eyes still on him, there was little Dex could do but nod. When he looked up, he found Seb had turned away from him and back to his work, his shoulders hunched and unforgiving.

Seb didn't look around as he spoke again. "The recipe is in the folder. Get the scales and start weighing."

Dex fetched the scales and the folder with a giant cake on the front that clearly denoted it as the dessert folder. He set them on the counter, opened the folder, and stared hard at the pages, hoping something familiar would jump out at him.

Seb appeared silently beside him. Up close, he seemed bigger than Dex remembered, but his unique vanilla scent was as intoxicating as it had ever been. "Get some self-raising flour from the dry store."

"Is that the blue one?"

"It says what they are on the packets."

Dex trudged to the dry store, but as luck would have it, another chef was already there and passed him the right flour without comment. By the time he got back to the counter, Seb had already started weighing out the ingredients, some with the scales, and some by eye. Dex watched with a fascination he remembered from watching Seb make fudge back in Padstow.

"Pass me that chocolate."

Dex picked up the bowl of broken-up chocolate and duly poured it into the saucepan Seb seemed to be mixing his ingredients in.

"What happened to your hands?"

"Hmm?"

"Did you burn them?"

Dex looked down at his hands. He'd forgotten the strange, scaly rash that had appeared a few hours after he'd cleaned the charcoal grill. "No. They're a bit funny from cleaning the grill."

"Did you use D9?" Seb took the pan from the counter and slid it onto the gas burner behind them. "You're supposed to wear gloves with that, and goggles. Did you read the bottle?"

Dex peered into the saucepan containing the slowly melting butter, sugar, and chocolate. "What goes in next?"

"Eggs." Seb retrieved a bowl of beaten eggs. "Wait until the chocolate is just about liquid, then take the pan off the heat and mix these in. I'll be back in a minute."

Seb disappeared, abandoning Dex with the pan of molten chocolate. For a moment, he was relieved, like he could breathe again, and then his heart felt the loss of Seb's presence beside him.

Fuck. How can he still do that, after all this time?

Dex didn't have a clue, and he spent the rest of the shift fluctuating between a desperate need to stand as close to Seb as possible and the real knowledge he'd stayed too long in Stoke Newington. Seb had found him, and by chance or not, it was only a matter of time before someone else did.

"How long are you going to keep this up?"

Dex glanced around, but Seb had spoken quietly. To anyone else, it looked like he was simply checking his work. "Keep what up?"

"This. I know it's been... a while, but I don't get it. Did I do something to upset you?"

Dex stared. "Upset me?"

73

"Why won't you talk to me?"

"What do you want me to say?"

Seb hissed though clenched teeth. Dex leaned back from the harsh, impatient sound until Seb finally sighed. "Meet me after work. I can't work with you like this. It's driving me fucking crazy."

CHAPTER THIRTEEN

Dex tried to slip away at the end of the hellish shift. He took a quick and necessary shower in the staff room upstairs, bypassed the bar where the rest of the staff had gathered, and snuck out the back door to find Seb waiting for him on the steps. Damn. Rick must've told him Dex never stayed for a drink.

Seb stood and inclined his head toward the street. "Come on. Let's get a beer."

His voice was hard, his face firm and unyielding. Dex had spent his whole life complying with the wishes and demands of others, and it felt natural to slink down the steps and follow Seb to the nearest pub.

He sat on a bar stool while Seb ordered drinks. He wanted to stand and be ready for an easy escape if the opportunity came up, but he was tired—bone-deep tired—from a day that had turned every facet of his new life upside down.

Seb slid a pint of something toward him and reached for his wallet. Dex found his balls at the last moment and paid the barman. Seb shot him a questioning look, and Dex scowled right back. He had money. He could buy his own bloody drink.

"This is a bit weird, eh?"

Dex swallowed a bitter mouthful of beer and considered Seb's question. He didn't like booze. He only drank it when someone told him to. "I didn't know you'd be here."

"Neither did I until a few days ago, and trust me, you were the last person I expected to see. How did you end up in London?"

Dex shrugged. Talking to Seb didn't feel as strange as he'd thought it would, but that was a question he couldn't answer, and a telling reminder that the sooner he moved on, the better.

"Rick really likes you. Thinks you've got promise."

"Best pot washer in town, that's me."

Dex's tone was dry. Seb frowned and shifted his position, leaning forward on the bar to face him. "You do more than that, Dex. I saw you in the kitchen today. You're really good, especially considering—"

"Considering what?"

Seb took a drink of his beer and set it down again with undue care. "You can't read, can you?"

"Can."

"I don't believe you."

Dex slid off his stool and shoved his hands into his pockets. He wasn't sure what he'd expected when Seb had ambushed him, but it wasn't this. So what if he couldn't bloody read? It wasn't like he'd ever been to school to learn.

Seb caught his arm. "Don't go, Dex. I'm sorry, okay? I won't tell anyone. I promise."

Seb's hand engulfed Dex's wrist, his touch as charged and heated as it had ever been. Dex felt his resolve melting, ebbing away until it was all he could do to fall back onto the bar stool. "I can read some," he said mutinously. "I can read numbers, and names. Knew the name of your shop, didn't I?"

"Can you write?"

"Never tried." Dex looked down. Lying to Seb felt all wrong. He'd heard the name of Seb's shop on the street, and the only name he could read was his own.

Seb was silent for a moment, then without warning, Dex felt his fingers brush through his shower-damp hair. "It really is brown. I thought it was just wet."

Dex fought for the strength to shy away from the soft gesture, but nothing happened. "The bleach grew out."

"It was dyed?"

"Couldn't you tell?" Dex had forgotten his brief stint as a blond was all Seb had ever known of him.

"No, not at all. You look totally different now. Not sure I would've recognized you without the scowl. You just about shocked the shit out of me. I... I thought I'd never see you again."

Dex chanced a glance up to gauge Seb's mood, to see if he was joking, but he wasn't even looking at him anymore. He was staring into his empty pint glass, looking as lost as Dex felt.

Dex pushed his own drink Seb's way. The whole day had been a mess from the moment he'd opened his eyes and emptied his stomach on his bedroom floor, but he hadn't stopped to think about how Seb might feel. Never had. "Why are you in London?"

"Sold the shop."

That made Dex sit up. He'd spent most of his time with Seb that summer watching him sweat blood to keep his inherited family business open. Back then, it had seemed to Dex that Seb would spend the rest of his days tied to his big copper pot. "Why?"

Seb shrugged and drank half of Dex's beer in one big swallow. "I was lonely... and bored. I've been making that bloody fudge since I was a nipper, and I felt like life was passing me by, you know?"

Dex didn't, but he nodded anyway. "Rick said he knew you before."

"I did my apprenticeship at his place in the city. We worked together for a few years, and when he called me up last week, it seemed like fate. The shop was off my hands, and I had nothing else lined up. Even the bloody cat had kicked the bucket. Besides, I like London. I never really wanted to leave."

"I like London too." The sentiment surprised Dex, but it was true. Kitchen work was hard and left him aching and tired, but he loved it. Loved the warmth from the ovens. The scent of the food in the air. For the first time since he'd crept out of Seb's bed last year, he felt safe and secure. The thought of leaving broke his heart all over again.

"If you're happy here, you should stay," Seb said, as though he could read Dex's thoughts. "Rick's a grumpy git, but he's a good man. He'll look after you."

"Don't need looking after."

Seb shook his head slightly. "Everyone needs looking after sometimes, even you. Is Rick feeding you? You look bigger."

"Bernie feeds me."

Seb smiled before an emotion Dex didn't recognize flickered over his face. "Where do you sleep?"

"In my room."

Dex didn't volunteer where, and Seb didn't ask. Instead, he bought another beer and got Dex something in a bottle that tasted like lemonade. "If we're going to work together, we need to figure this out."

"Figure what out?"

"This." Seb gestured between them. "I know you're not pleased to see me. I can see it in your face."

"It's not that."

"Then what?"

Dex took a swig from the bottle. The drink was sweet, and the sugar-laden fizz made his tongue feel loose. "I never meant to stay here so long."

Seb fiddled with the beer mat. Dex could see the cogs turning in his brain. "We can pretend it never happened, if that's what you want. I won't tell anyone."

Dex nodded slowly. "I don't want to pretend it never happened. I just…." He stopped and gathered his words. "I don't know what you want from me."

"Nothing. Dex, I came here to work. I won't even talk to you if you don't want me to."

"I don't want that."

"What *do* you want?"

Dex swallowed the last of the sherbet-flavoured drink. "I don't know."

And he didn't. He wanted Seb to leave him alone, to disappear into the night and never come back, but at the same time, he wanted to tunnel inside his jacket, wrap his arms around his strong body, and never let go. And he didn't understand either notion. Dex wanted to bang his head on the stick wooden bar. He'd spent much of his life afraid or apathetic, but he'd never felt either with Seb. That summer, Seb had brought Dex alive, shown him things he'd never imagined... had spent every moment they'd been apart dreaming of. Who the fuck was afraid of their *good* dreams?

Seb dropped his empty glass on the bar with a dull clatter. "You left me, Dex. I woke up, and you were gone, like you were a fucking dream. I tried everything to forget you, but I've thought about you every day ever since."

DEX COULDN'T sleep that night, taunted by memories of that summer and what had become of him after he'd left Padstow and accompanied Braden back to Hatfield. That year with Braden had been the darkest yet. The johns were meaner, more demanding, and brutal, and he'd had to do things he'd never imagined. Horrible things. Depraved things.

And he was scared too. Terrified. Surely it was only a matter of time before Braden tracked him down? The next morning, he packed up the few possessions he had—clothes, mainly, and a small knife Rick had given him—and walked to the bus stop. He wasn't altogether sure where he was going. The Oyster card Rick had given him meant he didn't have to buy a ticket, but he figured he'd stay on the bus until it went somewhere he didn't recognize, then get off and go back to hooking until he found something else.

He thought about leaving London altogether, but what was the point? He couldn't afford to go far, and the bustling city was probably the best place to hide.

"Hey, Dex!"

Dammit. Dex stopped a few meters from the bus stop and

turned to face Rick. It was seven in the morning. Rick didn't open the kitchen doors before eight. He lived above the restaurant. What was he even doing out here?

"Morning, lad. Glad I caught you. Listen, I need you to do me a favour. Bernie's out for the day, and I've got to run to the meat market. Can you take my key and let the boys into the kitchen?" He pushed a pile of cool metal into Dex's hand without waiting for an answer. "Cheers, mate. The alarm code is four-six-zero-eight. Just type it in when it prompts you."

And with that, Rick was gone, leaving Dex with the biggest set of keys he'd ever seen and instructions he could hardly comprehend. He'd also missed the bus, and it was rumbling away by the time he came to his senses. So much for his great escape.

He trudged his way to the restaurant, feeling like a puppet whose strings had been cut. It took him a while to find the right key, but the back door was easy enough to open. The intimidating alarm system was less accommodating. He could read numbers well enough, but the buttons on the alarm system looked different from playing cards, and the alarm got impatient and blasted him with a wall of sound so loud it made his teeth vibrate.

He breathed a sigh of relief when he finally managed to silence it, and then he leaned his head against the fire doors, letting the cool of the glass seep into him and calm his frazzled nerves.

"So you really can read numbers?"

Dex jumped and spun to face Seb, who was slouched in the kitchen doorway like he'd been there all along. Perhaps he had. "Told you I could, didn't I?"

Seb snorted, amused and noncommittal. "I need coffee before I can handle that chip on your shoulder."

He disappeared into the bar, and by the time Dex came down from the bathroom, he was at the dessert counter, setting out the oddest array of ingredients Dex had ever seen. So odd, he forgot himself and spoke first. "What are you making?"

"I'm not making anything. You are." Seb shot him a grin that made his knees weak. "Lemon yoghurt cake, with lemon thyme.

It's an American recipe, so it uses cup measurements, not the metric scales. Here, look at this. Does this make sense to you?"

Dex took the sheet of paper Seb passed him and squinted at the numbers and symbols on the page. Wait. They weren't symbols, they were pictures. Pictures of all the ingredients spread out on the counter.

Seb came around the counter. He was half a foot taller than Dex and had to lean down to see the page. "See, here are all the ingredients. It's an all-in-one batter. All you have to do is measure out the right quantities and turn the mixer on."

Dex frowned. Some of the combinations made perfect sense, but others were utter gibberish. "What does that mean?"

"Teaspoon." Seb reached for a set of strange metal spoons and pointed to the symbols on the handles. "This is a tablespoon, a teaspoon, half a teaspoon, and a quarter. See these numbers here?"

Dex could see them all right, but he wasn't sure he quite understood them. A wave of panic rushed up from his belly. If he got it wrong, all the ingredients would be wasted, and Seb would be angry. And so would Rick....

Seb touched his shoulder. "Just have a go, okay? I'll help you if you get stuck."

Dex reached for the lemons in the bowl, scrutinizing the picture someone, maybe even Seb, had drawn for him. "Just the skin, right?"

Seb smiled. "Right, the zest. We're going to make syrup with the juice. I'll show you when the cakes are in the oven."

The mixture turned out surprisingly well, or at least, Seb seemed to think so. He showed Dex how to line and grease the pans and set the oven to the right temperature, and then, while the cakes were baking, he guided him through boiling up the syrup to pour over the top.

During service, the cakes were Dex's responsibility. Seb shouted every time he needed one plated up, and by the end, Dex figured he could make some sense of the scribbled tickets he passed his way. Shame they sold out of the cake. He couldn't read for shit, but he knew enough to know the words he recognized today would look totally different tomorrow.

"You've got a blueprint now," Seb commented when service finally ended.

Dex glanced up from the sink. It wasn't his job to wash up anymore, but he couldn't seem to leave the mess for anyone else. "Blueprint for what?"

"For tomorrow. We served the lemon cake with blueberries today, we'll do a lime one with mango tomorrow, and orange and rhubarb at the weekend. It's essentially the same cake, just dressed up different."

Seb's choice of words felt familiar. "Like the fudge?"

A subtle flash passed through Seb's eyes. "Thought we weren't going to talk about that."

Dex shrugged and scrubbed a cake tin.

Seb hoisted himself onto the counter by the sink. "We need to think of a way to help you out. I can write all my recipes so you can follow them, but it won't work for the order tickets."

"You don't want me to help you anymore?" Dex's heart sank, and his resolve to get on the bus that morning felt like a distant memory, almost like it had been the thought of somebody else.

"The opposite, actually. I'm saying we need to teach you to read."

"We?"

"Yeah. I think you need to tell Rick. He's going to notice sooner or later. This way he can figure out how best to help you."

Dex frowned. "I can't tell him. He'll sack me."

"No, he won't. At worst, he'll keep you on desserts with me until you've learned the basics. You might not fancy that, but it's better than going onto main line and fucking up on there. Those guys will string you up before they bother to help you. They don't have the time."

Dex turned away and pulled his hands from the hot, soapy water. He dried his hands carefully, and when Seb didn't speak again, Dex assumed he'd walked away. Until he stepped back and collided with his solid chest.

"I got you something."

Dex took the white tube he held out and turned it over in his hands. It looked like toothpaste. "What is it?"

"Cream for the burns on your hands."

"Burns?"

In answer, Seb took his hands and pointed to the rash between his fingers. "These are chemical burns, Dex. You need to treat them or they'll get worse."

Dex's silence must've convinced him he lacked the intelligence to understand spoken English as well. Seb took the tube back and squeezed a bead of white cream from the end. He massaged the lotion into Dex's left hand. "Rub it in like this twice a day until the rash is gone."

Dex swallowed and thought he would faint until Rick cleared his throat from somewhere behind them.

"Don't mind me, boys. Seb, can I have a word?"

CHAPTER FOURTEEN

RICK SLAPPED a bundle of papers down on the bar. He'd ambushed Dex the moment he'd walked through the door later that day. "You're not the first lad I've had through here who never went to school, Dex. It's easy enough to fix, if that's what you want."

Dex chewed the inside of his cheek. Part of him was furious Seb had betrayed him, but he was mostly relieved. Seb was right: it was only a matter of time before Rick discovered he was an illiterate idiot. "How do you fix it?"

"There's two ways. We can get you down to the local college, or we can get someone to come here."

"Is it expensive?"

"Not really, but don't worry about that. We'll pay for it."

"Why?"

Rick rose and rounded the bar to refill his coffee mug. "It's the least we can do considering the peanuts we pay you. And the only reason I don't pay you properly through the books is because I get the feeling you don't really want me to. Am I right?"

The question seemed rhetorical, so Dex held his tongue, but Rick was right. He had no ID, bank accounts, or national insurance number. And he'd never told Rick his surname.

"Look at it like this." Rick sank back onto his favourite bar stool. "This way, I don't feel like I'm taking the piss out of you, and you get to add some more skills to your belt. It's an opportunity, lad. Take it while it's there."

Put like that, how could Dex refuse? "Okay."

"Okay." Rick grinned and flipped through the papers on the bar. "I had a woman come in and teach a few lads a couple of years ago. She was pretty good, but there's a place in Tottenham you could go to if you didn't want to do it here. It's an Irish centre, actually. They help a lot of Traveller kids there."

"What? No... no, I want to do it here."

"All right, lad, all right. I'll give her a ring and get back to you, okay? In the meantime, I think you better stay with Seb on puds for the next month or so. He's a good teacher, and he'll help you with this as well. That all sound good to you?"

Dex nodded and backed toward the door. The prospect of spending the next four weeks by Seb's side was equal parts thrilling and scary as hell, but he was done talking about himself, and the urge to bolt back to the kitchen was too strong to ignore. Rick let him go, and he spent the rest of the day trying to decipher Seb's instructions for the lime and mango cake. All things considered, it didn't turn out too bad.

Dex zipped up his coat against the frosty chill. It was early, barely seven, but the night before, Seb had decided he'd had enough of the kitchen and told him to meet him at the nearest Underground station in the morning to help him gather some specialty supplies.

Dex had never been on the Tube. He'd spent a lot of time in the Underground stations, but he'd never boarded an actual train. Seb didn't notice his wide-eyed hesitancy when he hustled him into a carriage. He seemed preoccupied with something on his phone, and Dex was content to slump in the seat next to him and watch the black tunnel whiz by the windows.

A little while later, the train jerked to a stop. Dex looked around, but as far as he could tell, they hadn't pulled into a station. He shifted in his seat. What had they stopped for? Was it like the buses when the inspectors got on and checked your tickets? Seb said his Oyster card was fine for the Tube, but what if he was wrong?

Seb squeezed his arm. "It's just a queue to get in the station. Won't be long."

He went back to his phone, but the scorching heat of his touch remained long after he'd withdrawn his hand.

Dex stared at his arm in consternation. Over the past few days, Seb had kept him so busy, he'd almost forgotten the haze of that summer hanging over them, but out in the real world, without the noise and chaos of the kitchen to distract him, it felt more real and intoxicating than ever.

"Come on. Let's go."

Dex blinked and realised the train had rumbled the last few yards into the station. He followed Seb off the train and looked up at the sign. "Where are we?"

"King's Cross, but we're getting another train to Angel. Come on, this way."

Dex followed him through the station and down the biggest escalator he'd ever seen. "Why are we going down again?"

"This line is really deep."

Oh.

They arrived in Angel ten minutes later, and after another trip on a grotesquely long escalator, Dex was relieved to get aboveground again. He trailed after Seb as he visited a few specialty shops. He kept his head down in most of them, but the chocolate shop smelled too good for him to resist chancing a furtive glance around.

Seb grinned and shoved a chocolate button into Dex's mouth. The surprise attack caught Dex off-guard, but the chocolate was good, *really* good, so he let it slide.

After the chocolate shop, Seb veered off toward a supermarket. Dex faltered. London was a diverse city, and the big green sign was the first shop he'd recognized. "I can't go in there."

Seb didn't hear him. Dex bit his lip and considered letting him go on without him, but he was carrying half of Seb's purchases, and he didn't want him to think he'd stolen them. "*Seb.*"

Seb froze and turned around slowly.

Dex didn't quite understand the expression in his face. He pointed to the sign. "I'm not allowed in there."

"What?" Seb frowned. "You're not allowed in Waitrose? Why not?"

Dex shrugged. He didn't really know the answer to that, he just knew he wasn't allowed in. "I'll wait here."

Seb's gaze flickered rapidly between him and the entrance to the shop, then comprehension dawned on his features. "Dex, it's illegal to ban people from shops based on their race. You can go wherever you want."

Dex shook his head and planted his feet on the pavement. Seb was a gorjer. He'd never understand. "I'm not *allowed* in there."

"Yes, you are. They don't profile customers at the front doors. I told you, it's illegal."

Dex didn't budge. Seb stared him down for a moment before he realised he wasn't going to win. He sighed and disappeared into the shop. Dex slunk over to the wall to wait for him. A dog was tied up outside. It was long-legged and wiry and reminded him of the lurchers his da used to keep before another family took them away. Leap, Ennis, and... Dex couldn't recall the name of the third, but he remembered crying himself to sleep every night after they were gone.

The journey back to Stoke Newington seemed to take longer than it had the first time round. The trains were busier too, and when they hit the aboveground lines, they had to stand. The rail track was bumpy and rough. The train jolted and Dex stumbled. Seb wrapped his arms around him, steadying him, and it took Dex a while to notice he never let go.

"WHAT ARE you doing now?"

Dex stepped into his battered trainers. "Putting my shoes on."

Seb sighed from the staff room doorway. "I didn't mean literally. Are you going straight home?"

Dex frowned. It was after midnight, and they'd only just cleaned the kitchen down. Where else would he go? "It's late."

"I know. Long day, eh? I'm bloody starving. Come on. Let's get some real food."

They headed out into the night. Seb didn't say much and Dex didn't say anything at all, but the quiet was lost in their surroundings. It was Saturday night, and the north London streets were alive with a heady buzz of energy. No one here went to bed before dawn.

After a while, Dex noticed they'd left the vibrancy of Stoke Newington behind and wandered into an altogether darker part of town. The air was heavy with the scent of spicy food, herbs, and a hint of danger. "Where are we?"

"Dalston. It's where the Turks live. See all these cutthroat barber shops?" Dex followed Seb's gaze. "Them and the kebab shops stay open all night. Have you got a quid?"

Dex fumbled in his pocket and pulled out a handful of change. He held out his hand and watched curiously as Seb helped himself to a few coins. "What are we getting that costs a quid?"

"Lahmacun," Seb answered, as though it was obvious. "Best shit in London. Lived on them when I was a student."

He ducked into a shop with a giant chunk of spinning meat in the window. To Dex, it looked like something from the dog food factory Braden used to sell his old horses to. Or a maypole from a horror film.

"Here you go."

Dex accepted a warm roll of wax paper. "What is it?"

"I told you. Lahmacun. Try it."

The glint in Seb's eyes was endearing and made him look like a young boy. Dex peeled back the paper and found soft white flatbread rolled up round a thin layer of warmly spiced minced meat. He took a bite. It was... amazing. Suspiciously amazing. "This cost a pound?"

"Yep. Always has, and probably always will. I used to have them for breakfast, lunch, and dinner back in the day."

Dex nodded around a mouthful of food. Half the roll was gone already, but he couldn't stop stuffing more in his mouth.

Seb watched him with a soft smile as he ate his own food. When Dex was done, he inclined his head toward the shop. "Want another one?"

Dex considered his answer and shook his head. He could probably eat another three, but he knew the more he ate, the more likely he was to wake up hungry, and he was still getting used to the fact that he could do something about it. Either that, or he was still waiting for the rug to be pulled out from under him.

They began walking again, though they didn't seem to be heading anywhere in particular. Seb finished his food and put their rubbish in a nearby bin. "Where's your place? Is it near here?"

Dex gestured back toward Stoke Newington. "It's not far."

"Is it a flat?"

"No, it's a hostel. Rick got me a room."

"St. Mary's?"

"Think so."

Seb didn't say anything, and after a while, his silence got under Dex's skin. He folded his arms over his chest and huffed out an annoyed puff of air. "Where do *you* live?"

Seb touched his shoulders lightly and turned him round, pointing to a huge utilitarian-type building on the other side of the road. "Right there. Come on. I'll show you."

It was a less impassioned plea than the last time Seb had invited him into his home, but fuelled by a full belly and a wave of emotion he didn't quite understand, Dex crossed the road and followed Seb into the building.

Seb's flat was on the fourth floor. The lift that took them to the uppermost floor was so tiny Dex had to stand practically on top of Seb, and it reminded him of the strange embrace they'd shared on the Tube a few weeks earlier. The door to Seb's flat was on a balcony that doubled as a walkway. Dex stared out at the city skyline as Seb led the way. At ground level, London was dirty and noisy, but up so high, the twinkling streetlights and spooky silence made it seem almost mystical.

"This is me." Seb opened a thick grey door and stood back. "Come on in."

Dex stepped inside. The heavy door slammed shut behind him. He swallowed his nerves and took in Seb's home.

Wow. His eyes widened and he felt his mouth fall open. He had sketchy memories of Seb's seaside cottage in Padstow—he'd had other things on his mind—but he was pretty certain it had been nothing like the ultramodern luxury of the converted ware-house flat. Shiny wooden floors. Weird pictures on the walls. There was even a metal spiral staircase that led up to another level.

Seb caught Dex's bemusement. "That's the bedroom. This is the living space and the kitchen. Bathroom is down the hall on the right. You want a beer?"

Dex shook his head. He really needed to tell Seb he didn't like beer.

"Here, have one of these, then. My sister left them here last weekend."

"Your sister?" Dex took the lurid blue bottle and took an experimental sip. It tasted a bit like the drink Seb had bought him the day he'd started at Rick's restaurant.

"Kelly lives in Farringdon. She pops over from time to time." Seb took his coat off, hung it over the railing of the spiral staircase, and flopped down on the sofa. He looked tired, and Dex didn't blame him. It had been a long day.

He drifted to the bookcase and looked at the neat rows of books, CDs, and DVDs. Despite his first tentative sessions with his teacher, Mel, the writing on them still meant nothing, but one DVD title caught his eye. "What's that?"

Seb glanced at the shelf and looked a little sheepish. "*Swiss Family Robinson.* I'd like to say it's my dad's, or even my grand-dad's, but it's mine."

Dex looked closer at the spine of the DVD. "I think my aunt

used to have that on video. Is that the one where they get ship-wrecked on an island and make bombs out of coconuts?"

Seb laughed. "Yeah, that's the one. I used to watch the big battle at the end over and over, until I got older and just freeze-framed on Fritz."

"The one with the curly hair?"

"Yep. He was hot. Probably still is. Want to watch it?"

Dex shrugged. If Seb wanted to, it was fine by him. It was his home, after all. He thought about heading back to the hostel, but Seb's softly lit living room was warm, and he didn't feel like facing the cold again yet.

"Take your coat off. I've got some Twiglets somewhere."

Seb fiddled around while Dex took off his coat and sat on the end of the sofa. A bowl of Marmite-flavoured corn twigs appeared in front of him, and the huge TV on the wall flickered on a moment later, bathing the room in a weird blue light until the familiar opening theme of the film replaced it.

Dex stared at the screen in wonder. The film was exactly how he remembered it, only bigger and brighter. The TV in his aunt's caravan had been tiny, its picture grainy and blurred. This was something else. He'd never seen anything like it.

Seb slid onto the other end of the couch, clicked the lamp off, and tucked his feet beneath him. "You'll get square eyes if you stare at it like that. Sit back and get comfy. You've got two hours to drink it all in."

Dex hadn't realised he'd leaned forward like a kid in a sweet shop. He glanced at Seb, who looked like he was about to fall asleep, and followed his lead, leaning back on the cushions and curling his legs beneath him.

He rested his head on his arm and watched the stormy ship-wreck unfold on the screen. His favourite part was when the Robinson family rescued the animals from the sea and built a new life for themselves on the uninhabited island, and he fell asleep to the sound of squabbling siblings and racing zebras.

CHAPTER FIFTEEN

DEX WOKE to a lukewarm cup of tea, a towel, and a crude sketch of a shower. He assumed it was meant to convey that he was welcome to use Seb's bathroom in his conspicuous absence, but not trusting his ability to read the digital clock on the DVD player, he gathered his shoes and fled.

Out of sync, Dex found himself at work two hours early. Seb didn't appear until 11:00 a.m. He winked at Dex, but neither man mentioned the night Dex had spent on his couch.

Later that night, after a *long* day at work, Seb handed him a paper-wrapped lahmacun. "Sorry I skipped out on you this morning. I had to sort something out."

"It was early, right?" Dex took a bite of his late-night supper. "I was in the kitchen by eight."

"Couldn't sleep?"

"No. I didn't know...." *Idiot*. Was he really about to admit he was too stupid to tell time? That he only got to work on time each day by asking the hostel warden? "Thanks for letting me stay."

Seb grinned through a mouthful of food. "Anytime. You looked really sweet curled up on the sofa. I didn't want to wake you."

Dex balled up his paper and flicked it into a nearby bin. They were sitting on a bench by a bus stop in Dalston. He liked Dalston. It was rough, but around them, the borough's nocturnal residents went about their business without so much as glancing their way, and Dex felt safe on her spice-scented streets.

"What are you going to do with your day off?"

Dex frowned. He'd forgotten about that. It seemed Rick had decided he no longer needed him to work seven days a week. His Friday-morning roll of cash would remain the same, but starting tomorrow, he'd have every Monday off. A whole day and night alone in the hostel. He couldn't wait... not. "Dunno."

"I get Mondays off too. It's the quietest day of the week. Providing I leave plenty of prep, Rick can handle it. Do you want to get a drink or something?"

"A drink?"

Seb slid off the bench and ambled to the bin so Dex couldn't see his face. "A cuppa, or a pint or something. Unless you're sick of the sight of me."

"No."

Seb turned back. "No, you don't want a drink? Or no, you're not sick of me?"

"I'm not sick of you."

"Good." Seb came back to the bench, but remained on his feet. "Do you have a phone?"

"Rick gave me one, but I haven't turned it on yet." Dex didn't add that he was waiting until he could read the instructions for himself. He hadn't told anyone that. Besides, why did he need a phone? Who would he call?

"You can find your way back to my place, right? I'll be home all day. Come over anytime and we'll do something." Seb nudged Dex's shoulder. "Night, Dex."

Seb walked away. He was halfway down the road before Dex found his tongue.

"Hey, Seb?"

"Yeah?"

"It's flat twenty-three, right?"

Seb smiled, his eyes crinkling up at the sides. "That's right. Press number four in the lift."

THE FOLLOWING day, it only took a few hours of kicking about his empty bedroom for Dex to give in and go looking for Seb. Cold and lonely, he *missed* Seb. They'd spent every day together for a couple of weeks now, and Dex had grown used to his soothing company. Even when Seb was yelling at waiters, he still had gentle words for Dex. Gentle words that made him feel safe and warm. Not like the barren cold of his hostel room.

The warmth buzzing in his veins increased when he saw the chef hat hanging on Seb's front door, guiding his way. He knocked. Seb pulled open the door, covered in the white dust and a broad smile. "All right, mate? Wasn't sure you'd show."

"Why have you got flour all over you?"

If Seb was offended by Dex's greeting, he didn't show it. Instead, he waited for him to kick off his shoes, and then beckoned him into the kitchen.

Dex stared at the mess on Seb's sleek, modern counters. There was stuff everywhere, and he was clearly cooking up a storm. "It's your day off."

Seb shrugged and poured what looked like eggs into a precarious well in the centre of a huge mound of flour. "I know, but I want to make Chelsea Buns for the old ladies' lunch tomorrow, and the dough is better proofed overnight. Can you pass me the dough hook for the mixer?"

Dex ventured farther into the kitchen. He knew what a dough hook was. The planet-sized mixer at the restaurant had one. "Where is it?"

"Cupboard by the bread bin."

It took a few moments, given Dex was looking for something far bigger, but eventually, he retrieved the white enamel dough hook and attached it to Seb's domestic mixer. "Why's your mixer pink?"

"Because my brother thinks he's bloody hilarious."

"Your brother?"

"Yeah, Ezra. I told him I was gay when I was fifteen, and he's been buying me pink shit ever since." Seb scooped up a huge ball of dough he'd created from the mess of flour and eggs and dumped it in the stainless steel bowl of the mixer. Dex could see it said "kitchen" on the logo, but he didn't know the other word. "Turn it on to speed six, and grab me a beer from the fridge, will you? There's some WKD in there for you."

Seb put his hands in the sink without waiting to see if Dex understood his instructions, and began washing his hands. Dex turned the mixer on and opened the fridge, eyeing the other untouched ingredients on the countertop. "What else are you making?"

"Pizza." Seb poured his can of beer into a glass. "There's enough dough left over, and I figured we could both use some real food."

Dex couldn't argue with that. He'd missed Bernie bringing him his usual morning butty, and he hadn't eaten since their shared supper at the bus stop. "How do you make pizza?"

Seb grinned. "Give the mixer ten minutes, and I'll show you."

And, over the course of several drinks, that's just what Seb did. He taught Dex how to make the biggest pizza he'd ever seen, and after that, how to fold the dough in half to make a stuffed pasty he said was called a calzone.

"How do you know so much about pizza?"

Seb wiped his mouth and pushed his plate away. "The dough part is basic pastry skills, but I learned how to spin it when I spent a few months in Naples."

"Where's that?"

"Italy. I travelled around Europe when I was training. Naples, Paris, Barcelona, Prague. Seems like a lifetime ago now, but I've still got some tricks."

Dex swallowed his last bite of calzone. "How old were you?"

"Nineteen." Seb shot Dex a strange look. "How old are *you*?"

Dex squirmed. "Twenty."

Seb narrowed his eyes. "Don't lie to me again. Rick said you told him you're nineteen."

"I was *then*."

"When was your birthday?"

Dex thought hard. He knew it had passed, but it had been so long since he'd marked the occasion, he often forgot all about it. "Last… Thursday, maybe?"

Silence. Dex averted his gaze. He'd forgotten he'd lied to Seb. When they'd met that summer in Padstow, he'd told Seb he was twenty-two. By that reckoning, he should've been pushing twenty-four by now. Like anyone would ever believe that.

Seb nudged his shoulder. Dex glanced up to find him just a hairbreadth away. He could smell basil and garlic on him, mixed with the vanilla that was uniquely Seb. The intoxicating scent took him back to a kitchen even smaller than this one, a kitchen rattled by the ire of a summer storm and the tattoo of his own stampeding heart.

Dex sucked in a breath as Seb stared him down. That night, he'd felt the warmth of Seb behind him burn into a heat too consuming to ignore. For the first time in his life, he'd asked, no, *begged* another man to take him and fuck him until there was nothing else in the world.

Dex swallowed. Did he want that again? Could he *bear* that again?

Seb bit down on his lip so hard Dex thought he'd bite it right off, and then he rubbed some stray flour from Dex's face with the hem of his T-shirt and sighed. "Come on. Let's go out."

SEB SLID another bottle across the table. "They didn't have the blue one."

Dex shrugged and tilted the bottle of bright orange fizz to his lips. It looked like Lucozade and tasted like soap, but he was about four drinks past caring.

He glanced around, taking in the dilapidated interior of the grotty Tottenham pub. It felt familiar, like the seedy pubs Braden used to visit... while he left Dex sitting outside on the curb.

The unpleasant nostalgia had made him nervous, and to calm the monster in his belly, he'd gulped back every drink Seb and Damon, another chef from the restaurant, had pushed his way. A sensible strategy, it seemed, as now he was so drunk he could think of nothing but Seb's knee wedged against his thigh under the tiny wooden table.

Seb seemed equally inebriated, though he was more extroverted about it than Dex. Dex had noticed that over the last few weeks. In contrast to the solitary creature he'd appeared to be in Cornwall, Seb was always smiling and laughing. Everyone loved him. Seb was everybody's friend, and the only friend Dex had ever had.

"You're not going to drink that Irn Bru shit, are you?"

Dex glanced at Damon and placed the half-empty bottle carefully on the beer mat in front of him. "Might as well."

Damon sniggered. "You're going to be hanging in the morning. That orange crap stays with you. Hey, Seb. Are you going to dick around on your phone all night or play some darts with me?"

Seb rolled his eyes and shoved his phone in his pocket. He seemed annoyed, though Dex couldn't be sure. "Really? Again?" He cast his gaze in Dex's direction. "Damon's the worst darts player in the history of the world, and that's saying something, considering how bad I am. Want to play?"

Dex had played darts before, a long time ago with Mikey when he was feeling charitable. The rules escaped him, but he was fairly sure the idea was to hit the tiny red dot in the centre of the board.

Easy enough, but maybe not, judging by Seb's raised eyebrow when Dex hit his mark for the fourth time.

"Okay. If you're going to hit a ton-eighty every time, it's going to be a pretty short game. You ever played Around the Clock?"

Dex shook his head, glad the concentration of aiming the dart had shifted his introspective, drunken haze. "Is that like Pontoon?"

"Not quite." Seb put his arm around his shoulders and explained the rules of a convoluted game Dex had no hope of understanding. "Just aim where I tell you," Seb said in the end.

Damon scowled. "Oh, I see. Two against one. Nice. Is this because I work the grill instead of poncey desserts? Arseholes."

The gripe was good-humoured and Damon's grin wide, but Dex still felt a tremor of apprehension run through him. A tingle. Like he could feel unwelcome eyes all over him.

He shook off the sensation and took the darts from Damon's extended hand. The only eyes on him were Seb's, and his whirlpool gaze felt like Dex's own secret world. A world where nothing and no one could touch him. No one but Seb.

Dex let the dart fly, aiming where Seb pointed. Taking turns with Damon, he hit his mark, once, twice, three times, until Damon threw down his darts in defeat. "Bloody hell. I give up. One more round in here before we hit the Dolphin?"

Seb nodded. Dex shrugged too, though he was pretty sure he'd reached his capacity for sugary carbonated drinks. His belly felt full and bubbly, and for once, it had nothing to do with Seb grasping his elbow or pushing his hair back from his face. No. This time, he was simply so drunk he could hardly comprehend the low rumble of Seb's voice in his ear or the yearning look in his eyes.

Or the louder voice in the back of his head telling him the drink Damon passed his way was one drink too many.

He took a swallow of the red drink. A bitter taste hit his tongue, and it was all he could do not to spit it all over the table. "What *is* that?"

"Absinthe and cranberry. My missus drinks it all the time."

Seb swiped the glass from Dex's hand. "Don't give him that. Donna would drink weed killer if you put it in a glass with a cherry on top."

Dex didn't know if he was annoyed or relieved. Annoyed that

Seb thought he needed babysitting, or relieved he didn't have to drink the red drink that tasted like petrol. He opened his mouth, but to say what, he'd never be sure, as Damon cut him off. He reached around Dex and punched Seb's shoulder.

"Look lively, mate. Your freaky boyfriend's heading this way."

CHAPTER SIXTEEN

SILENCE. SEB glared at Damon then scowled again at whoever was approaching their table. "Ex-boyfriend," he said gruffly. "I finished with him yesterday. Fuck's sake. I'll be back in a minute."

Damon let out a grunt that seemed approving, but over the noise of the raucous pub, it was hard to tell.

With Seb gone, Dex swiped back his absinthe-laced juice and knocked back a long swallow. *Seb has a boyfriend. A boyfriend. Seb. Seb has a boyfriend. Seb has a boyfriend.* Nope. It didn't sound right, no matter how many times he said it. He took another pull of absinthe. Drained the glass. Fuck. He needed a piss.

Damon paid him no heed as he rose from his seat and made his way to the toilets. He'd learned the words "ladies" and "gents" the day before in his literacy lesson, but these ones had the pictures on... the stick figures with squares and triangles to denote the sex.

He relieved himself, sniggering a little at the notion that the triangle-shaped female figure looked like she was wearing the cape of a superhero, and stopped at the bar on his way back to buy beer for Damon and Seb. He couldn't think of anything to get himself, so he didn't bother, and Damon didn't seem to notice when he set two sloshy pints of lager down on the table.

Seb was still MIA. Dex glanced around, feeling a tremor of nerves break through his drunken haze. He wasn't supposed to go in pubs, or bars or nightclubs. His place was outside, waiting on Braden, or peddling whatever white powder or pill he'd stuffed into his pockets. He'd followed Seb inside because he'd follow Seb to the end of the earth, but now he was gone and it didn't feel right. *He* didn't feel right.

"Hope he really has ditched that twat."

"Hmm?" Dex rescued his much-abused thumbnail from his teeth. "Seb's boyfriend?"

"*Ex*," Damon replied sardonically. "At least, I hope so. Have you ever met Andy? The bloke's a weirdo. I swear down, he only eats chips and kebabs. Can you imagine Seb stuck with a bloke like that? Talk about repressed."

Dex could only nod. Most of Damon's words went over his head, but he was right about one thing. Seb couldn't be with someone who didn't share, or at least appreciate, his passion for his job. Seb bitched and moaned about work all the time, but it didn't stop him from taking it home with him, working long into the night, and starting all over again at the crack of dawn.

"He made pizza today."

Damon grinned over his pint. "Yeah, he's pretty good at that. I do a better barbecue, though. Wait until summer, and we'll get some dustbin lids out on that fancy balcony of his. Get lagered up and get some birds round."

Birds? Oh yeah. Damon likes girls.

Seb dropped silently into his seat. He looked annoyed but not upset, and Dex was glad he hadn't turned around to see what his mysterious boyfriend—*ex*-boyfriend—looked like.

Damon slid one of the pints Seb's way. "All sorted?"

Seb scowled before he seemed to chance a glance at Dex. "Yeah. Daft wanker. We were only together a few months. The way he's harping on, you'd think we were getting a fecking divorce."

Damon snorted. "Never trust a man who doesn't like onions."

"Onions?" Dex was lost.

"Yeah. Onions are, like, the backbone of every dish. If you don't like 'em, you don't like nothin'."

Dex frowned, mystified, and Seb's sudden bark of laughter broke the awkward air that had settled over the table.

"Jesus, Damon. There's more to life than bloody onions. Come on. Fuck this shit. Let's drink up and go to the Dolphin."

Seb and Damon finished their drinks and hustled Dex down the street to another pub. The pub was noisier than the last one, crowded and rowdy. Dex topped up his drunken stupor with a few more bottles of blue WKD, but eventually, the shouting and jostling bodies became too much for him. When his heart began beating so fast he thought he'd be sick, he saw an opportunity and made his escape.

He was halfway down the road when Seb caught up with him.

"Hey, slow down. Where are you going?"

"Home?" Dex offered, though in his current state, he wasn't entirely sure, and the fact that he hadn't registered Seb coming up behind him scared the shit out of him. Fuck. He could've been anyone. He could've been Braden.

"Do you know the way?"

Dex jerked his head to the left, leaving his equilibrium spinning, and for once, not from the evil concoction of Seb's dark hair and brooding blue eyes, perfectly silhouetted by the murky London sky. "That way."

"Dex, we're in Tottenham. Stoke Newington's this way." Seb turned Dex a full 180. "Unless you want to walk all the way to Shoreditch."

Oh. He should've been embarrassed, or at least annoyed, but he was too drunk to care. "Guess I'll go this way, then."

Seb snorted and fell into step beside him. "You're a funny pisshead."

"I'm not pissed."

"Liar. You're as lashed as me."

Dex tripped over his own feet. "So?"

"So nothing. Are you hungry?"

"No." And for once, it was true. His stomach was so full of booze and bubbles he couldn't envision it having room for anything else ever again.

"Me neither. Let's go home."

Seb spoke with a slur and slung his arm around Dex's shoulders. The gesture was light and affectionate, and steadied Dex, helping find his feet again. By the time they reached Dalston, he felt mildly more sober and too exhausted to go on. He spotted the bench where he and Seb usually ate their midnight supper and drifted over to it. He sank down and put his head in his hands. His legs felt weird. He didn't want to walk anymore.

Seb dropped down beside him. His arm had slipped from Dex's shoulders when he'd pulled away to sit on the bench, but the closeness of him now was enough.

Or was it?

Dex raised his head and leaned back on the bench, and it seemed only natural to lean into Seb, to absorb his warmth as a buffer against the icy December air.

"Tired?"

Dex's only response was a grunt. He was so weary he could fall asleep right there. Perhaps he would, if Seb was willing to be his pillow. Perhaps he'd sleep here anyway, even if Seb left and went home. Went home to his fancy flat and his....

Wait a minute. Dex jerked upright. "Where's your boyfriend?"

Seb sighed. "Not you too. *Ex*-boyfriend. I'm not with him anymore."

"Why not?"

"Because he's annoying, and I don't want to be. What do you care?"

Dex shrugged and considered his answer. He didn't know much about boyfriends and girlfriends. Where he came from, you were either a child or married. Or nothing, like him. "When did you break up with him?"

"Sunday morning."

"Why?"

Seb rolled his eyes before his expression faded to something a little more sombre. "You really want to know?"

"Asked you, didn't I?"

Seb shifted so he was facing Dex. "I met Andy this summer, and we were just shagging, really. Nothing to write home about, but he was fucking clingy. Coming to London seemed a good way to get rid of him. I felt bad about it for a while... until I saw you. Then I saw you asleep on my couch and I just knew."

"Knew what?"

"Knew that even if you don't want me right now, I can't be with anyone else."

Dex didn't know what to say. He stared at Seb, bit his lip, and felt the rowdy Dalston streets fade to nothing. "I can't be a boyfriend. I can't do that."

"I'm not asking you to, Dex. You asked me a question, and I answered it."

Dex rubbed his eyes with the heels of his hands. He felt dazed and confused, and a little bit sick. Perhaps a sign he should call it a night and go home, before he talked himself into trouble. He rose unsteadily to his feet.

Seb stood too and grabbed his hand. "Hey. It's late, and cold. Why don't you kip on my couch? Save walking home."

It wasn't all that far to the hostel—ten minutes at most—but Seb was right. It was late and Dex was tired. The clean-smelling upholstery of Seb's couch was too tempting to pass up. "Okay."

They walked to Seb's flat in silence until Seb let them in and bypassed the lift. "So you can find the stairs," he explained. "In case it's ever broken."

It seemed a silly reason to trek up four flights of steps, but Dex held his tongue. It was Seb's flat. If Seb wanted to climb the stairs, who was he to argue? Still, he was relieved when Seb finally unlocked his heavy front door. The warmth of his home hit Dex like a sucker punch, and he all but fell inside.

Dex shrugged out of his coat and toed off his shoes. Seb hung their coats in a small cupboard by the door and gestured down the hall. "Go use the bathroom. I'll get you something to sleep in."

"What? Oh, no. It's fine. I can sleep in my clothes."

"I know you can. You just don't have to. Go take a hot shower. I'll leave some clothes outside."

Dex obediently made his way to the bathroom. He'd been in there the day before to use the toilet, but he hadn't considered the huge showerhead hanging over the bath. He stared at it now, taking in the complex dial. The shower at work was fairly simple —blue for cold, red for hot. It was just a matter of jiggling it until he found a temperature he could stand. This one seemed far more intricate, even without the added complication of written instructions.

He pulled his T-shirt and hoodie over his head, then stepped out of his jeans. Then, clad only in his underwear, he took a chance and turned the dial clockwise into the red section. Nothing happened. He tried again, twisting it this way and that, until he remembered the shower in Braden's caravan needed the tap turned on before it would work.

It did the trick. He turned the hot tap halfway and water burst out of the showerhead, blasting him like a water cannon. Startled, he jumped back, feeling his heart quicken. He stood stock-still a moment before he worked up the courage to hold his hand under the spray. The water was hot and hard and stung his skin, but it felt *good*. Encouraged, Dex shed his remaining clothes and climbed into the bath.

There was something exhilarating about being naked and alone in a place that was all Seb, about rubbing soap and shampoo into his body that smelled of him. Stolen and exciting, like Seb was seeping into his skin, and no one knew it but him. Dex washed carefully, taking his time and breathing it all in before the water became too hot to bear.

He switched the shower off on his second attempt and stepped out of the bath. True to his word, Seb had left some clothes outside the bathroom door. Dex retrieved them and pulled them on before he set about cleaning up the bathroom.

A little while later, he ventured down the hall in search of Seb, clutching his own clothes close to his chest. He found Seb on the sofa, sitting in the dark with the TV on so low Dex could barely hear it. A blanket and a pillow lay stacked at the other end of the couch.

Seb greeted him with an easy grin. "Better?"

Dex nodded. He did feel better. Still drunk, but pleasantly so, rather than dizzyingly out of his head. "What are you watching?"

Seb patted the couch beside him. *The Naked Chef*, back when he was geeky and hot, rather than the preachy lard arse he is now."

"More cooking?"

Seb hummed lazily. "Yeah. Never stops. Here." He handed Dex the pillow. "Get comfy."

Dex considered his options. Seb was at the very end of the sofa, beer can in hand, his legs stretched out. His posture was relaxed and at ease, but Dex wanted more. He wanted to climb into Seb's lap and kiss his stubbled cheek, tug on his lips with his teeth and bury his hands in his short, dark hair.

He wanted to lose himself in Seb's gaze and never be found.

Seb turned his lips up in a wry smile. "What do you want, Dex?"

Dex tugged on his knee. "Lie down."

Seb shifted onto his back and straightened his legs. "Like this?"

Dex crawled over Seb and wedged the pillow under his head. He thought on it some more then lay down and wriggled until he was under Seb's arm with his head on his chest. After a moment's deliberation, he hooked his leg over Seb's for good measure. "Like this."

Seb laughed and set his beer can on the floor. He wrapped his arm around Dex. "Fair enough."

Seb shut off the TV and darkness enveloped them. Dex pressed his face into Seb's chest and inhaled the scent he'd caught a whisper of in the bathroom. Perhaps he'd regret this in the morning, but for now, he didn't care.

Seb draped a blanket over him and carded his fingers through Dex's hair. "Dex?"

Dex opened his eyes and looked up. "Yeah?"

"Good night."

Dex smiled, and in answer stretched up and pressed his lips to Seb's in a soft, hesitant kiss. "Good night, Seb."

CHAPTER SEVENTEEN

DEX WOKE with a start, his face mashed into Seb's chest and the rest of Seb's body wrapped protectively round him like a cocoon. His head hurt and his stomach felt like he'd been kicked by a horse, but the warmth of Seb's arms felt amazing.

And so did the pulsing, throbbing heat pressed against his thigh.

For a moment, Dex didn't dare move, breathe, or even blink, and then a wave of exhausted nausea swept over him and he found himself burrowing closer to Seb as though he could climb inside him and escape the fast-growing hangover brewing deep in his bones.

He woke again sometime later to Seb rubbing his back. "All right?"

Dex blinked, both relieved and disappointed to find the dick pressed into his leg had retreated back where it came from. "What time is it?"

"Eight. You've got your lesson with Mel at nine, haven't you?"

Dex sat up and scrubbed his hands down his face. It was Tuesday, the day he had a two-hour reading lesson before his workday even started. Dammit. Why hadn't Seb reminded him of that *before* he'd drunk his body weight in lurid fizzy booze? "I need to go home."

"What for? You can use the bathroom here. Stay awhile and rest. You'll need it if you're going to get through today."

"It's not that. I need to get my washing so I can do it at work."

"Oh." Seb was silent a moment. He looked tired and rough, and Dex could almost see the effort it took him to think coherently. "How about you grab a shower and a cuppa here, then you go to work while I fetch the washing from your place?"

"You want to go to my place?" Dex wasn't sure about that. He kept his room clean and tidy, and his dirty clothes were stacked in one of Bernie's big linen bags by the door, but glancing around Seb's sleek, polished flat, he wasn't sure he wanted him to see the sparse reality of his life at the hostel.

"I've been there before, Dex. I know what it's like."

Dex sat up again. Somehow, his head had dropped back to Seb's chest. "What? Why did you go there?"

"Last time I lived in London, my head chef used to donate leftovers to the homeless shelters around the city. I took some food there once."

Dex clambered off the couch, stumbling over the too-long legs of his borrowed tracksuit bottoms. He didn't have much in his life to be proud of, but it bothered him that Seb knew just how lowly he was. "Where did I put my clothes?"

"Over there."

Seb inclined his head toward the coffee table. Dex frowned. He didn't remember putting them there. "I need to go."

Seb didn't argue, and he didn't reiterate his offer to go to the hostel either. He watched Dex scramble around for his things with an unreadable expression on his face, and when Dex emerged from the bathroom dressed in his own clothes, he met him by the front door with a travel mug of hot, sweet tea.

"See you later."

Dex ran home, changed his clothes, and dragged his bag of washing up the road to the restaurant. His detour had made him later than usual, and after loading his things into the machine, he was just in time for his literacy lesson.

He usually enjoyed his sessions with Mel. Reading was hard,

and writing near on impossible, but he could see with his own eyes he was making progress. Not today, though. Today, the words on the page seemed to blur into a migraine-inducing riddle. Mel lost patience in the end and sent him back to the kitchen an hour early.

After setting up the dishwasher—a habit he'd yet to break—Dex wandered over to the dessert section, noting Seb and the Chelsea Bun dough they'd made the day before had yet to appear. He retrieved Seb's weekly planner and flicked through until he came to the right day, but aside from the words "bun" and "lunch," he could decipher little from the handwritten plans for the day.

He rubbed his belly. The headache was fading, but his insides still felt empty and raw, like he was hungry, or sick, or both.

"Morning."

Seb dumped a big plastic box down on the counter. Dex jumped but found himself distracted by the ball of Chelsea Bun dough billowing over the sides of a glass bowl. "That's huge."

Seb smirked, though Dex could see his eyes were drawn and weary. "Amazing, eh? Give me a minute to get a brew, and I'll show you how to punch it down."

Punch it down?

Seb ambled off to the bar and reappeared a few minutes later with two mugs of tea. He passed Dex one, along with a bag of sweets and a paper-wrapped package from his box of tricks. "Cheese and Marmite. Pink shrimps and fried eggs."

Dex's mouth watered. He felt like death, but cheese and Marmite? Food of the gods, and no one made it better than Seb. "What have you got?"

"Jam sarnies and cola bottles. Don't let me eat them all before lunch. I'm going to need the sugar this afternoon. Pass me that bloody dough. Let's get this over with."

Dex stuffed half a sandwich in his mouth and watched, fascinated, as Seb knocked the air out of the dough with his fists and turned it out onto the floured counter. By the time it was stuffed with spiced raisins and rolled into spiralled buns, it didn't look anything like the gloopy mess Dex had walked into the previous afternoon.

Seb wrapped them in cling film. "Right. They just need to proof on top of the steamer for an hour, then they can go in the oven. Do you know what cake you're making today?"

Dex picked up the baking tray loaded with the buns. "Lemon drizzle."

"You've got the recipe squared away?"

"Think so."

"Okay. Good. I've got to pop out for a while. I'll be back before service starts. If you need anything, ask Rick."

Seb took his bandana off and tossed it on top of the microwave. His tone was friendly enough, but he didn't look happy. Dex took the buns to the steamer and slid them into the warm space where the air leaked out. When he came back, Seb was still there, staring into space.

"Okay?"

"Hmm? Oh yeah. Apart from hanging out of my arse, at least. Hey, can I ask you something?"

Dex nodded and reached for the second half of his sandwich. He felt better already.

"What does gorjer mean?"

He dropped the sandwich like a stone. "What?"

"Gorjer. You kept muttering it in your sleep. Is it someone you know?"

Dex waited a moment for his tongue to detach from the roof of his mouth. He'd never talked in his sleep before, at least not that he knew of. He was pretty sure Braden would've beaten it out of him. "You're a gorjer. I'm a Traveller."

Seb stared at him, then shook his head and gathered some paperwork from the file he kept in the counter drawer. "See you in a bit."

He disappeared, leaving Dex to finish the lunchtime prep alone, and when he came back just before service started, he remained pensive and quiet for the rest of the afternoon. Dex didn't mind. Battling through a busy service with a raging hangover was hard enough without maintaining conversation, but when the lunch rush was over and it was time to clean up and get ready for dinner, the sombre silence began to get under his skin. He was about ready to scream by the time Rick summoned him into the bar.

He crossed the kitchen in a world of his own and pushed open the bar door with little thought. A wall of noise hit him, and he looked up to see every soul he worked with, from cleaner to chef to waitress, staring at him, smiling, and singing a song he knew he should recognize.

The scene made little sense, and he didn't even realise they were singing to him until Bernie appeared in front of him, brandishing a big blue cake with four lit candles on top.

"Happy birthday! Sorry it's a bit late, sweetie. Make a wish!"

Mystified, Dex followed her prompt and blew out the candles. His colleagues treated him to a round of applause before they began to disperse, armed with slices of cake dispensed by Bernie.

Dex watched them go with wide eyes until he caught sight of Seb loitering at the back of the bar. He let Bernie hug him before he crossed the room and poked him in the ribs. "What the bloody hell was that?"

Unfazed, Seb chuckled. "I don't remember much from last night, but I *do* remember that we missed your birthday. There's no escape, Dex. Bernie makes everyone a cake, even me, the pastry chef.... Oh, don't give me that look."

"What look?"

Seb folded his arms across his chest, and looked Dex in the eye with an expression that made his knees feel weak. "*That* look. You deserve a normal life, Dex. A life where your friends treat you right. Wind your neck in and let them."

DEX FROWNED. "It's not my birthday anymore. It's not even close."

"Shut your face." Seb kept his attention on the big pot he had bubbling on the stove in his flat. "A bit of crappy cake does not a birthday make."

"I'll tell Bernie you called her cake crappy."

"No, you won't."

Okay, Dex probably wouldn't, but he still didn't see why Seb was cooking him a special dinner two weeks after a birthday he'd never celebrated in the first place. Though he wasn't about to complain about spending his day off in Seb's nice, warm flat. "What are you cooking?"

"Beef cobbler. My mum still makes it for my birthday every year, even in Spain."

"Spain?"

"Yeah. My parents retired out there a few years ago, but she still manages to get all the ingredients."

"Do you miss your ma?"

Seb shot him a strange look. "Not really. I moved away when I was eighteen, so I'm used to seeing her just a few times a year." Seb looked like he wanted to say something else, but he didn't. Instead, he held up the spoon for Dex to taste. "Like it?"

Of course he liked it. Seb was a magician. "Can I help?"

"Nope. You're going to sit right there and let me look after you. No whinging."

Seb's attempt at stern was endearing, and ineffective given the humour lightening his gaze, but Dex stayed put all the same. He loved watching Seb cook. Often, he seemed to throw things together with little thought, but if Dex looked close enough, the tiny frown creasing his forehead or the tip of his tongue poking through his teeth gave him away.

"What did you eat on your last birthday?"

Some dirty john's cock. "Pot Noodle?"

Seb made one of those noises that reminded Dex of his mad old aunt and tipped the meat sauce he'd made into a chipped baking dish. Like most of Seb's kitchen equipment, the dish was a girlie shade of pink. "Did your brother buy you that?"

"Hmm? Oh yeah. Of course he did. Wish I could chuck it out, but it's the best dish I have." Seb threw a handful of grated cheese into a sticky dough mix he was working by hand. "Pass me the chives from the fridge."

"Thought I wasn't allowed to help."

"Don't be an arse. Come on, I need to roll these scones out before the butter gets too warm."

Dex was familiar with the science of ice-cold butter in baking. Seb had taught him to make pastry and recited a list of other recipes the theory applied to. He retrieved the chopped herbs from the fridge and obediently added them to Seb's bowl.

A little while later, he sat back on his stool and rubbed his rounded abdomen. Of a list that was ever growing, beef cobbler was officially his new favourite food. Meat, gravy, and cheesy scones—life didn't get much better than that.

Seb wouldn't let him wash up. "Not today. It's your day off. Relax."

"It's your day off too," Dex grumbled.

"Bite me."

If only. Dex was glad Seb had his back to him. It had been nearly a week since he'd woken up in Seb's arms, their bodies... their cocks... pressed together in a tangled pile of heat, but he'd thought of little else. Seb hadn't mentioned it, but something had changed between them. The slight awkwardness that'd plagued them had faded away and been replaced with a casual affection that was almost easy.

Almost, because just the lightest touch from Seb—a shoulder squeeze, a brush of hands—was enough to light Dex on fire.

"Do you want pudding?"

"You're not cooking anything else for me."

Seb laughed. "Easy, mate. I brought home the leftover banoffee pie you made yesterday. Don't tell me you don't want any. I saw you eyeing it up last night."

Dex let him have that one. Toffee, bananas, biscuits, and cream. Who wouldn't want to eat that? "Okay, but let me get it. Please?"

Seb relented with an easy grin and ruffled Dex's too-long hair. "Bring it in the living room. We can watch a DVD or something."

Dex slid off his stool and busied himself retrieving the leftover pie from the fridge and serving a big slice onto the only plate he could find. He took the pie and two forks into the living room and found Seb sitting on the floor with his back to the couch, thumbing through a big leather book.

"What are you doing?"

"Looking for a picture of Ezra. Thought you might like to put a face to a name."

Seb found the page he was looking for and beckoned Dex closer, gesturing for him to leave the pie on the table and take a seat in front of him. Dex hesitated only a moment before folding himself to sit between Seb's bent legs, caged in his arms with his back to his chest. "That's your brother?"

"Yep." Seb swept Dex's hair back from his face, and when Dex didn't squirm, he rested his chin on his shoulder. "He's two years older than me and two years younger than our sister, Kelly."

Dex stared at the slightly older, less good-looking version of Seb. The man had lighter eyes and hair, and his face was free of Seb's perpetual stubble. "Your sister who lives in London?"

"Farringdon. She was over here yesterday, actually. Can't you see how clean this place is?"

"Your place is always clean," Dex said absently, flicking through the pages of the photo album and taking in image after image of a smiling, happy family.

"Only because Kelly comes by and does all my housework when I'm at the restaurant. I'm having dinner with her next week. You should come."

"Why?"

Seb huffed out a tiny, heated puff of air that made the hair on Dex's neck stand on end. "Why not?"

Dex didn't have an answer. Instead, he nestled closer to Seb's chest and let the sound of his rich voice wash over him, lulling him into a sated and contented daze. In turn, Seb played with his hair and told him stories of family holidays in the south of France.

He perked up a little when Seb came to pictures of his old fudge shop in Padstow. He touched a faded picture of Seb's whole family posing on the pavement by the rickety old sign. "Do you miss it?"

"The shop? No, not really. I only kept it going out of some misplaced obligation to my grandpa. I was all kinds of relieved when my dad told me he would've much preferred to see me living it up in the city than tied to a small-town shop all by myself. Besides, the rest of them turned their backs on it, so why not me?"

Dex nodded slowly. Seb had told him before that life in the shop bored him to tears, that he was lonely. He hadn't seen it back when he'd first met Seb… first saw him drifting through the cobbled Cornish streets, weary and sticky from a day behind the fudge pan, but after watching him thrive in Rick's busy kitchen, it all made perfect sense. "I'm glad you came."

Seb rubbed his scruffy cheek against Dex. Stroked his face and brushed his thumb over his lips. "Came where, London?"

"Yeah."

Seb's answering kiss was sweetly terrifying. He took Dex's face in his large hands and kissed him again and again until Dex opened his mouth and kissed him back with everything he had, grounded only by the solid warmth of Seb's chest beneath his clutching fingers.

The kiss went on and on until Seb pulled away, lifted Dex like he was nothing, and laid him down on the sofa. Then he stopped. Stopped dead, like he'd come to his senses. "Shit. I'm sorry. You make me crazy, you know that?"

Dex wriggled and arched his back, unwittingly seeking friction for his dick. "I don't mind."

"You said you didn't want this."

"No, I didn't."

Seb drew back and let out a shaky breath. "I don't under—"

Dex kissed him, kissed him fiercely, hard and demanding. "I never said that." Another kiss. "I said I couldn't be your boyfriend. I don't know how."

Seb cupped Dex's chin, calming the fire of the kiss to a gentle roar. "Do you want to learn?"

"Maybe." Dex slid his hands under Seb's T-shirt, resisting his natural instinct to break Seb's intense stare and cast his gaze down. "I want to kiss you some more."

Seb smiled and kissed the tip of his nose, laughing at his answering frown. "We can do that, but I don't expect anything from you. I want to be with you, but only if it's what you want, and you can take as long as you like to figure it out. I'm not going anywhere."

Dex knew it was true. He didn't know much about much, but every fibber of his being told him his faith in Seb was well placed. Trouble was, he didn't know how to compute the rising desperation he had to be as close to him as possible into a reality he understood. "I should go."

"You're probably right." Seb rolled from the couch and hauled Dex to his feet. "See you in the morning?"

Dex chewed on his tingling lip. "See you in the morning."

He left the flat. A cold breeze buffeted him as he made his way to the lift. Seb called his name as the button turned red.

"Hey, Dex?" Dex turned, and Seb's smile was blinding. "Happy birthday."

CHAPTER EIGHTEEN

THE OVEN timer beeped. Dex switched it off and squinted at the torn notebook page Seb had left out for him.

Check tart is set. Remove from oven. Switch oven off.

Dex opened the oven door and eyed the treacle tart, shaking the tray the way Seb had shown him. The centre of the sticky breadcrumb mix wobbled slightly, but knowing it would continue to cook as it cooled, he took a chance and removed it from the oven.

The tart was last on his mental list of prep, and now that it was out and on the cooling racks, he found himself with nothing to do. Restless, he drummed his fingers on the stainless-steel countertop, missing Seb and his annoying, cheerful banter. He'd taken the day off to meet his siblings for lunch, leaving Dex to handle a busy December-afternoon service on his own. Rick had programmed the ticket machine to print single-word orders—tart, cake, pie, mousse—but Dex was still anxious, so anxious he couldn't keep still.

What would he do if a ticket came through he couldn't decipher? Or a waitress came through and left him a note? Mistakes were expensive, and he didn't want to spend his precious cash paying for fuckups.

He cleaned the already spotless dessert section from top to

bottom. Seb remained on his mind as he got down on his hands and knees and cleaned beneath the units. It had been a week since they'd wound up kissing on his couch, and since then, it felt like they'd done nothing but kiss at any opportunity they got. After work. During work, when they took a break between services on quiet days. Sometimes even before work, when Dex fell asleep on Seb's sofa the night before.

The kisses were magical... and petrifying. Seb never pushed Dex to go further, but God, Dex wished he would. Then sometimes, he didn't. Couldn't bear to even think of it. Seb had fucked his brains out back in Padstow, but the prospect of anything more than those sweetly volatile kisses scared the shit out of him.

Yeah, because maybe then Seb will remember you're nothing but a dirty little whore.

Dex felt sick. He didn't think of Braden as much anymore, and in some ways, that made it worse, and it caught him off guard when he did. Fuck. He wished Seb would come back, but knowing that wouldn't happen anytime before dinner, he threw himself into the needless cleaning with even more verve than before.

Damon appeared as Dex was wiping down the counters just one more time. He helped himself to one of Seb's specialty knives. "All right, mate? Surviving without Seb? You look stressed."

"I'm okay." Dex took a moment to hide his scowl. Stressed. Yeah, that was the word of the day, and the tiny slip of paper burning a hole in his pocket wasn't helping. He'd been mystified when Bernie had appeared waving a biscuit tin filled with folded slips of paper, and even her explanation of buying a present for whichever colleague he picked out didn't make much sense to him.

"It's just a Secret Santa, Dex. Don't look so serious."

Right. If only that were true. Naturally, he'd picked out Seb's name, and now he had to think of a present fit for Seb *and* venture into a shop to buy it. A bonehead task for a gorjer, but not for him.

"Earth to Dex?"

Dex blinked and Damon passed him a ticket. The rest of the

kitchen was already in full flight, but by nature, the dessert counter didn't get going until well after twelve. He studied the ticket. One chocolate mousse and three treacle tarts. He let out a measured breath. Easy enough. He could do that.

The next order wasn't so simple. A waitress hurried in and scribbled a note at the bottom of the ticket. Dex called her back. "What does that say, miss?"

"Pouring cream, instead of whipped. We have little jugs of it by the coffee station, remember?"

He didn't, because he rarely thought to get himself a hot drink, and the derision in the girl's eyes stung. She thought he was stupid. But what could he do? It wasn't like she was wrong.

The rest of service passed without incident, but it was exhausting, and when Seb finally appeared at five o'clock and sent Dex home for a rare night off, for once, Dex found himself more than willing to go. Until he remembered his Christmas shopping task, at least.

He took a shower, got changed, and set off for Kingsland High Street with grim determination. Most of the shops were Turkish barbers or restaurants, but he'd seen something a few days ago that had caught his eye, and, more importantly, had the price displayed next to it in big pink writing.

It began to rain as he walked along the bustling pavement. He shivered and wrapped his arms around himself. He didn't look up until he came to the tiny accessory shop stuck in his mind. Then his courage failed him. He couldn't read the poster stuck to the door—he didn't even recognize the letters—but to him, a sign on the door meant just one thing: he wasn't allowed in.

Dex stopped dead in the middle of the pavement, ignoring the jostling elbows of the people who passed him. Frustrations clawed at his belly. He could see what he wanted to buy hanging in the window—a bandana, black with a pink skull-and-cross-bones pattern. Seb always wore bandanas in the kitchen, even at home. Never a hat like Rick, a skull cap like Dex, or a baseball cap like the cheerful Pakistani pot washer whose name Dex could never remember. He wore a black chef jacket too, from time to time, and the pink tied in perfectly with the pink accessories that littered the kitchen of his Dalston flat.

Dammit. Dex *wanted* that bandana.

He dug his nails into his palms and looked down at his trainers. Bernie had washed them, way back when he'd first started at the restaurant. They'd come out whiter than they'd ever been, and without the mud of a caravan site to tramp through every day, they'd stayed that way. His clothes were clean, and so was he.

No one will know.

Was that really true? It was time to find out.

Dex steeled himself and walked into the shop. No one noticed, not even the shopkeeper. Dex chewed on his lip, confused. That wasn't how it went. He'd followed his ma into a shop in Kilkenny once, and a man had set his dogs on them.

Seeing no dogs, he sidled up to the bandana display and unhooked the one he wanted. The display was close to the till, and it was almost too easy to pass it to the shopkeeper with a handful of coins. The transaction was swift and silent. The shopkeeper held out the paper bag with a curt nod. Dex took it and fled the shop.

He ran all the way home to the hostel until he was safe in his room. Inside, he locked his door and stood against it a moment, breathless, his heart slowing to a normal rhythm. He'd done it... bought his first ever Christmas present. Question was, what the hell did he do with it now?

DEX WOKE later that night to a knock on his locked hostel room door. Yawning, he rolled from the mattress and padded across the room, assuming it was one of a regular parade of nighttime disturbances. It was common practice for hostel residents to bang on each other's doors at all hours, looking for cigarettes, rizlas, and sometimes money. Dex always answered, scared they'd kick the door right down, and tonight was no different, though the knocking was less exuberant than he was used to.

Seb greeted him with a lopsided smile. "Hey."

Dex rubbed his eyes, half-convinced he was seeing things. "What are you doing here?"

"Looking for my partner in crime. Service wasn't the same without you."

"Are you drunk?"

Seb shrugged and leaned on the doorframe. "A bit. No one bought me dinner from the kebab shop to line my belly. Are you going to invite me in?"

Dex stood back and let Seb push himself lackadaisically off the doorframe and amble into his room. He let the door swing shut and crossed his arms over his chest, defiant. His room was basic and sparse, but neat and clean. Cleaner, probably, than Seb's swanky flat.

Seb turned in a slow circle, taking in the bare mattress, battered wooden chair, and utilitarian metal shelves that served as Dex's wardrobe. "Like what you've done with the place."

"Very funny."

"I'm serious. It's not what I pictured in my head."

Dex wasn't sure he wanted to know what Seb had imagined. Lacking any better ideas, he shuffled back to his rudimentary bed and sat down. Seb hovered above him, looking down at him with an expression Dex couldn't quite decipher. "You can sit down if you want."

Seb dropped down beside him, leaving a small space between them. Dex closed the gap, drawn by the warmth of Seb's strong body.

"Where's your duvet?"

"Hmm?"

"Your duvet." Seb slipped his arm round Dex's shoulders. "And your pillow?"

"Don't have one."

"What? Dex, it's December. What keeps you warm at night?"

"My coat."

Seb stared at him, his merry gaze suddenly sober and grave.

He took a breath, but whatever he wanted to say was interrupted by a loud bang that startled them both.

Dex recovered first and rose to open the door. Seb tried to tug him back down. "What are you doing?"

"What do you think?" Dex reclaimed his hand and stomped to the door. The acne-scarred face of his immediate neighbour greeted him, as did the pungent smell of piss and booze.

"Dexy, my boy. Have ya got any skag, mate? I just need a little bit, man. Just a taste to get some shut-eye. I'll pay ya back, lad."

"Sorry, Tomo. I haven't got any. Do you want some crisps instead?"

After bartering for a while, Tomo accepted his obligatory bag of Skips and moved on to bang on the next door, no doubt hoping to exchange the loot for something more appealing to him. Dex shut the door. He turned around and found Seb right behind him.

"Why did you answer the door?"

"Why wouldn't I?"

"Because it's dangerous," Seb snapped. "This whole place is a fucking pit of drugs and scum. What if that junkie geezer comes back with some of his mates?"

"He hasn't got any mates." Dex stepped around Seb, feeling an invisible barrier spring up between them—the barrier that reminded him of his true place in the world. He'd expected it eventually, but it had slipped his mind somehow over the past few weeks, and the defensive anger in his veins surprised him. "What's it to you?"

"This place is shit."

"Shit for you, maybe," Dex retorted. "It's the nicest place I've ever lived. Sorry it's not good enough for you."

Seb's eyes widened. "Good enough for me? Are you taking the piss?" He crossed the room with one long stride and caught Dex's chin in his hand. "Dex, this place isn't good enough for *you*."

"Yes, it is." Dex shrugged out of Seb's grasp and stumbled backward. He sank down on the edge of the mattress. He didn't have it in him to fight with Seb, but he wanted to scream. The hostel *was* good enough for him... too good, because without it, where would he be? Sucking cock at the bus stop down the road.

Seb knelt in front of him. "Dex." He stopped and took a deep breath. "Dex, I don't care where you came from, or how shitty you perceive yourself to be. I can't live with myself while you're laying your head here every night. Come home with me. Sleep on my couch, in my bed, whatever. Just don't make me leave you here. Please."

Déjà vu swept over Dex. They'd had this conversation before, more than once, and each time, Dex had resisted. Each and every time until that summer storm had hit the Cornish coast and collided with the knowledge that Braden was on his way to take him back to Hatfield—back to the caravan site, to Mikey and to hooking. Back to making *real* money, after Braden's failed venture on the Cornish seafronts. "I don't want you to feel sorry for me."

"I don't, Dex. I just... I can't stop thinking about you. I *want* you with me. Fuck, I just want *you*. Come home with me. Please?"

CHAPTER NINETEEN

GENTLE HANDS shook Dex awake. He rolled over in the big, clean-scented bed and found Seb right there. "Wha...?"

"Rick called. Eddie's off sick, so one of us has to go in." Dex started to sit up, but Seb eased him back down. "I'll go. I'm awake, anyway. Stay here and sleep. I'll see you later."

Dex tilted his face for a kiss that swept sweetly through his bones. It felt good... really good, like he wasn't really awake kind of good. He lay back on the thick pillows and watched Seb disappear down the spiral staircase that connected his bedroom to the rest of the flat. He heard the shower switch on, and then the fridge rattle, but didn't move until he heard the front door bang a few minutes later.

Satisfied he was alone, Dex sat up. There wasn't much to Seb's bedroom—just another big TV, a cupboard built into the wall, and, of course, his bed. Dex dipped his head and pressed his face into the covers bunched around his bent knees. They smelled like Seb and fresh-cut grass. They smelled *amazing*, still, even after three whole nights to get used to it.

Three nights. Three nights out of the seven Dex had spent at Seb's place. At first, he'd resisted the call of Seb's bedroom, but the lure of his arms had proved too strong, and Dex was gone now, lost to the magic of sleeping with Seb's lips at his neck and his body curved around him, sheltering him, shielding him. Now he didn't know how he'd ever slept without him.

Dex lay down and curled up in a ball. It felt strange to be in the bed without Seb, but he was tired. There were only a few days left before Christmas, and the restaurant was crazy busy. Some nights, he didn't leave the kitchen before midnight, and last night, he'd still been there at two in the morning. He let his eyelids droop and drifted back to sleep, not waking until Seb dropped a kiss on his cheek sometime later.

"You went back to sleep, eh?"

"You told me to." Dex sat up, noting the tiny square of London sky he could see through the skylight in the ceiling had turned from morning grey to a distinctly dusk-like navy blue. Oops. It seemed the bed had magical powers, even without Seb stretched out behind him.

"You don't have to do everything I say, Dex."

"Hmm?"

Seb's grave expression puzzled Dex... puzzled him and got under his skin. It didn't suit Seb's face. Seb was a happy person. He smiled all the time, and the pensive look in his eyes was all wrong.

Dex couldn't bear it. He kissed Seb, kissed him with all he had, until Seb was in the bed and beneath him, tugging at the hem of his T-shirt. Dex pulled it over his head and stripped Seb of his before he could change his mind.

Then he faltered, finding himself above Seb once more, straddling him in a position of control he'd never been in before. He stared at Seb, and Seb stared back, his eyes wide as he took in Dex's bare chest... a chest that seemed too thin and pale in contrast to Seb's strong, curved muscles.

Dex took his hands from Seb, but Seb caught him before he could fold his arms around himself.

"Don't do that. God, don't do that. Look at your skin... it's perfect." Seb ghosted his fingertips up Dex's smooth abdomen and up over his hairless chest. "I didn't get to look at you like this before. Sometimes, it feels like it was a dream."

Dex trembled. Seb had said those words before, in that dingy bar the day he'd barged back into his life. Dex had disregarded them then, perhaps afraid to believe he could be a dream Seb could possibly want, but he believed it now.

Seb slid his hands down Dex's ribcage and to his hips, grinding their bodies together in a light, slow circle. Dex gasped, feeling the thick outline of Seb's hard cock press into him. He'd forgotten this, forgotten how big Seb was.

He put his hands on Seb's chest, felt the thud of his heart through his palms, and pushed back, seeking the friction that made his eyes roll. He moaned... no, whimpered, and did it again and again and again.

Beneath him, Seb groaned and tightened his grip on Dex's hips. "Come up here." Dex's eyes flew open. Seb pushed at the waistband of his borrowed sweatpants. "Take these off."

Dex stripped and straddled Seb's chest, his dick inches from Seb's mouth. *Oh God, oh God.* He remembered this too... the way Seb had fucked him until he could take no more, then laid him flat and blown him until Dex was screaming, on the inside, at least.

Seb pushed on Dex's back and guided him into his mouth. Dex fell forward and gripped the frame of the bed, giving in to the instinct to roll his hips forward. Sensation overwhelmed him. His breath caught and his skin burned and tingled like he was crawling deliciously out of his skin.

Dex put his hand on Seb's head and wove his fingers into his hair. For long minutes, he was caught between the sweet, hot heat of Seb's tongue and the probing twist of the warm, wet fingers he slipped inside him. *Curl them, God, please curl them.* Seb curled his fingers. Dex convulsed from his head to the tips of his toes, arched his back, and came in Seb's mouth.

Seb held him in place until he was done, tormenting him with his magical tongue until Dex begged him to stop.

Seb released him and maneuverer him like he weighed nothing. He laid Dex down and pulled him close. Dex felt him hard against his thigh.

Shit. You forgot about him.

Dex pulled away from Seb's kiss. "You can fuck me if you want."

Seb smirked. "What if I want you to fuck me?"

"Why would you want that?"

There was a beat of silence before Seb shrugged. "When I asked you 'top or bottom' back in Padstow, you hesitated. I thought you did both. It doesn't matter."

Top or bottom.

Dex thought back to the moment Seb had bent him over the counter in the kitchen of his Cornwall cottage and eased so gently inside him. The sensation had blown his mind… shattered it into a million pieces. Could he do that for Seb? Make him feel like that? Would he even know where to start?

Not a chance.

"Dex. It's fine. Don't worry about it." Seb shifted so Dex could no longer feel his dick, hard and waiting, and pushed Dex's sweat-damp hair out of his face. "This only goes as far as you want it to, okay? It's not why I asked you to come here."

Dex finally regained sensation in his limbs and propped himself up on his elbows. He felt strange—disconnected from his body and the reality of the day. "What time is it?"

"Have a look." Seb held out his phone so Dex could read the digits on the screen.

Dex squinted and let the numbers click into place. "Five o'clock? Really?"

"Yep. You've been in bed all day. Might as well stay here now. Want to get a pizza and watch a film?"

"Can we have mushrooms on it?"

Seb grinned. "Whatever you want."

———

"Merry Christmas, Dex."

Dex's hand trembled, threatening the neat line of whipped cream he was piping on the cake he'd baked for the special Christmas lunch service. He scowled at Seb. It was the third time he'd walked past him, brushed his fingertips across the base of his spine, and whispered in his ear, and the third time Dex had nearly fucked up his cake. Christmas Day meant little to him, but the simmering buzz of Seb beside him—every smile, wink, and loaded brush of skin—meant everything.

He finished up the chocolate cake and regarded it with a critical eye. It was the first recipe he'd devised and cooked all on his own, and Seb had picked a hell of a day to make him do it.

"You know how to bake a cake, Dex. You don't need my help."

Tosser. Still, all things considered, the cake didn't look too bad. In fact, it looked pretty damn good, at least according to Rick, who'd brought him a glass of something pink and fizzy a little while earlier. Apparently, it was tradition for the kitchen staff to drink their way through the Christmas Day service, and Dex wasn't going to argue with that. He liked drunk Seb. Drunk Seb was a lot of fun.

Service passed in a blur of laughter and fizzy wine. It was the most relaxed shift Dex had ever worked, and he felt deflated when it was over. Then he remembered he still had to write Seb's name on his present.

He slipped away to the staff room and retrieved the paper bag containing the bandana from his locker. The bag was green, so he figured he didn't have to find some wrapping paper, but there was no way he could get away with leaving the gift nameless.

He pulled his literacy book and a pencil from the locker and sat down on the floor, flicking through the book to find the right letters. The S and B were simple enough, but the E gave him a little more trouble. He held the finished result up to the light and glared at it with even more scrutiny than he had the cake. It was legible, just.

Bernie stuck her head round the door. "There you are. Do you have your present for the Secret Santa? We're going to do it in a minute, before people start to go home."

Dex stood and relinquished the green paper bag. Bernie knew without looking at his scrawl that it was intended for Seb, but she looked anyway and smiled.

"Would you look at that? He'll be so proud of you when he sees it."

"It's supposed to be a secret."

Bernie ruffled his hair. "Trust me, sweetie, he'll know."

Yeah, by the illiterate scribble.... "Are you giving it to him now?"

"Yep. Get changed and come down so you can get yours too."

Dex opened and shut his mouth, words dying in his throat as Bernie left him to it. It hadn't occurred to him someone had picked *his* name out of the tin.

He changed and made his way downstairs. It seemed everyone and his dog had crowded into the bar. Dex slipped in unnoticed and took a seat in the corner beside Damon. Seb joined them a few minutes later with a tray of drinks, and then it was time for Rick to do his much talked-about impression of Father Christmas.

It wasn't as funny as Dex had been led to believe, and he didn't pay much attention to the festivities until his name was called. He got up and accepted the floppy silver-wrapped parcel and took it back to his seat.

Seb nudged him. "Open it."

Oh. Carefully, Dex peeled away the shiny wrapping paper. A grey beanie hat and matching gloves fell into his lap. He turned the gloves over in his hands. They were thick and warm and lined with fleece. The sort of gloves he'd dreamed about when he'd slept on the streets of London all those months ago. The sort of gloves he'd dreamed of his whole life.

"Do you like them?"

Dex nodded. "They're like blankets."

Seb smiled, but said no more and headed up to the bar to retrieve his own gift. He returned with the green paper bag a few minutes later and set it, unopened, on the table beside Dex's hat and gloves.

Damon eyed it curiously. "Not going to open it? Can't be any worse than the set of teacups some knobhead got me."

"Later. I want to get pissed while Rick's paying."

It seemed a sensible plan, given the way Rick was handing out drinks. Dex sat back in his seat, absorbed the warmth of Seb beside him, and took it all in. He was tired, and before long, more than a little drunk, but beneath it all lurked an emotion he wasn't familiar with. He felt content and safe… happy, maybe, and as the night wore on, the sensation became more at home in his bones. Like it belonged. Like *he* belonged.

Later that evening, he found himself outside with Rick while he smoked a cigarette. Seb was inside, talking to his family in Spain on his phone, except he wasn't talking to them in a way that made sense to Dex. He'd gotten the shock of his life when Seb's sister appeared on the screen and called him by name. It had scared the shit out of him, and after a quick, hesitant wave, he'd made an excuse and followed Rick outside.

"Don't blame yer, son," Rick said gruffly through a lungful of smoke. "Leave them to that bloody bollocks."

Dex reached for the broom leaning against the storage shed and absently swept a few spent cigarette ends into a neat little pile.

Rick's chuckle rumbled through the frosty night air. "Leave it, kid. It's Christmas Day. All this'll still be here tomorrow."

Dex set the broom aside and hoisted himself up on a disused wooden table. A companionable silence fell over them, but Dex wasn't fazed. He often found himself alone with Rick, and the burly chef was a man of few words.

Not tonight, though. Tonight it seemed a whole day of drinking on the job had gone to Rick's head. "So, how're you doing, lad? Getting on okay?"

Dex nodded and tucked his hands under his arms, wishing he'd brought his new gloves outside. "I'm good."

"That you are. Bit of luck for both of us you just so happened to be passing by that day, eh? Kitchen would feel bloody strange without you now. How's the literacy going?"

"Good… I think. I can write some stuff now."

Rick smiled and looked up at the sky. "So I saw."

On cue, Seb appeared at the back door, the green paper bag in his left hand. Rick shot him a knowing look and shuffled back inside.

"So…." Seb let the word hang.

Dex stared at him, entranced by the reflection of the shimmering stars in his eyes. "So."

Seb held up the paper-concealed bandana. "You wrote my name."

"Did I?"

"Yeah, you did, and I'm so proud of you I could squeeze the bloody life out of you."

"You're drunk." Dex glanced at the open back door, but there was little need. Most of the staff had gone home, and all evening, Rick and Bernie had seemed to know there was something between him and Seb.

"Can I open it?"

Dex shrugged. "That's the point, isn't it?"

"Touché." Seb unfolded the bag and peeked inside. "Oh wow. Is this what I think it is?"

"Maybe." Dex watched, nervous as Seb shook out the bandana and held it up to the soft orange haze of the streetlight illuminating the bin yard. He'd never bought a present before. What if Seb hated it?

Seb moved, his large frame a blur of shadows. He put his hands on Dex and tilted his face until their eyes met. "I love it. It's perfect. Thank you."

Dex's response was cut off by a kiss, a lighter kiss than he'd grown used to of late, but his head swam nonetheless.

Seb broke away with a grin. "Funny how that worked out, eh? Do you really like that hat? I didn't know what to get you. You're an awkward little sod."

"You bought my present?"

"Yeah. I think Bernie engineered it that way, but I'm not complaining. I know you wouldn't let me buy you anything otherwise."

Dex rolled his eyes. "I don't need you to buy me things. I can buy my own."

"So why don't you? You need a coat, and something to sleep in."

Dex tilted his head, enjoying the sensation of Seb nuzzling his neck. "What's wrong with my coat?"

"It's too thin. Like you."

"How'dya know I'm too thin? Maybe God made me this way."

Seb smirked, and pursed his lips like he was trying to contain himself.

"What?" Dex scowled and squirmed in his arms. "Say it."

Seb shrugged. "I've seen your dick, Dex. You'll have to eat a lot more cake to grow into *that*."

Dex should've been annoyed, but he wasn't. He turned in Seb's arms and reached up to kiss him, hard, until he pulled away and said, "I can buy my own stuff."

"Do it, then." Seb kissed him again, once, twice, and once more. "Monday. Let's go shopping."

CHAPTER TWENTY

DEX WOKE first. It was Monday morning, New Year's Eve, and the first of two whole days he and Seb had to themselves. Rick had relatives descending from the north, and he'd shut the restaurant to host a rowdy family party. Dex rolled over with a wry grin. He'd seen Bernie's sisters arriving on a minibus from Liverpool. That party was going to be *loud*.

He sat up and rubbed his eyes, oddly alert given the hour he'd crawled into bed the night before, and especially considering the amount of time he'd spent exploring Seb's naked body before they'd gone to sleep. He peeked under the duvet. Yep. Seb was still naked. *Happy days.*

Shame Dex's bladder wasn't man enough to let him appreciate the sight for long. He slipped from the bed, pulled on some clothes, and slid down the swirly metal banister like a kid in a play park. He relieved himself, and washed up before padding barefoot into Seb's kitchen. Waking up before Seb was a rare thing, and he'd never made him breakfast before. In fact, he'd never seen anyone cook for Seb.

He considered the contents of Seb's fridge. Beer, milk, eggs, and, bizarrely, raspberries. Pancakes—the thick ones with fruit and syrup. He could make those, right? He knew Seb well enough to know his cupboards were well stocked with a gazillion varieties of flour and sugar.

It didn't take long. A cup of flour, the same of milk, and an egg. The raspberries crushed with a teaspoon of golden sugar. Drenched in syrup from the squeezy bottle, the whole dish looked pretty good. Dex set it aside and quickly cleaned the kitchen, washed the pans in the sink, and loaded the dishwasher. Then, armed with a cup of tea, he took his loot back to bed.

He found Seb still asleep, sprawled on his back with his arm flung over his head. He'd kicked the covers away, and his torso was bare right down to the duvet bunched at his waist. The scene stopped Dex in his tracks. Seb was amazing to look at when he was awake—animated and beautiful… passionate—but asleep? Dex couldn't look away.

He set the plate on the bedside table and crawled back into bed, casting his gaze down Seb's body. He took in his solid chest and rippled abdomen. Closer inspection revealed the small scar on his belly from a burst appendix a few years back… a tiny blemish that, when traced with Dex's tongue, made Seb curl his toes and shiver all over.

"What are you staring at?"

Dex started.

Seb chuckled and squeezed his leg, his eyes bright and laughing. "You're dressed. Did I sleep through my alarm?"

"You don't need your alarm today, remember? And I got up early… earlier than you, at least."

Seb rolled over and put his head in Dex's lap. "That's not like you. Couldn't sleep?"

"No, I was just awake." Dex pushed his fingers into Seb's silky hair, enjoying the sensation of Seb leaning on him. "I made you breakfast."

"Breakfast?" Seb cracked an eye open. "I've been trying to get you in my kitchen for weeks. What changed your mind?"

You've had me in my kitchen…. Dex ducked his head, his cheeks heating up as an image of that bloody summer flashed into his mind again. Fuck. Would it ever stop? "Thought you might be hungry after last night. We forgot to eat dinner."

"What did you make?"

"Pancakes. Like the banana ones you made last week, but, um, without the bananas." Dex handed Seb the plate and chewed on his lip. Seb inspected his cooking all the time at work, but this felt different… like the world would end if Seb didn't like it.

Seb took a bite of his breakfast. "Wow. These are great. I've got a recipe for sticky toffee pancakes with dates and caramel sauce. Not for breakfast, though. After dinner with ice cream. We can make them tomorrow, if you want."

Relieved, Dex rolled his eyes. Seb and his damn cooking. The man seemed to think of little else.

Dex burrowed back into the bed and curled into Seb's side while he inhaled his breakfast. Awake he may have been, but being in bed with Seb—with *naked* Seb—was the best thing ever.

"Are you still up for shopping today?"

Dex groaned. "I thought you were joking about that."

"Nope." Seb wiped his mouth and set his empty plate aside. "It's Kelly's birthday next week, and I want to buy some books in the sales. I was going to go to Oxford Street, but you don't have to come if you don't want to."

"Want" was a very strong word, but Dex didn't fancy spending the day alone. He arched his back, stretched, and tried his best to look enthusiastic. "I'll come."

"You look like a snake when you do that." Seb smiled and kissed Dex's T-shirt-covered chest. "Come on. Let's go."

OXFORD STREET. Dex stared at the sign, *reading* the words and letting them sink into his brain. He'd been here before. To the left was a shop doorway where he'd laid his head, and somewhere below his feet was the Underground station where he'd turned his first trick without Braden's guiding iron fist.

Oblivious, Seb tugged on his elbow. "This way. I need to go to

Monsoon for Kelly's present, then I want to go to the big H&M. You'll like the stuff in there. It's cheap and cool."

Yeah, 'cause that's me. "You don't have to pull me everywhere."

Seb protested with a roll of his eyes and yanked on Dex's hand until he fell into step beside him.

The streets were as crowded and terrifying as Dex remembered them. He kept his head down as he walked along, catching the eye of the occasional vagrant begging at the side of the road. Most of them didn't connect—too far gone from whatever had driven them to live on the streets—but from time to time, the hollow stare of one would linger, would penetrate his soul and remind him his place by Seb's side wasn't really his place at all. *"… dirty whore…."*

"What are you buying Kelly?"

"A handbag or something." Seb pulled a crumpled magazine page from his pocket. "Think she figures being gay means I give a shit." He stopped outside a shop. "This is the place. Are you coming in?"

Dex wanted to refuse. The shop was high class, refined, and teeming with women—all things that terrified him—but Seb was holding his hand, and he didn't want to let go.

He stuck close to Seb as they wove their way to the back of the shop. Seb was taller than him, heavier and wider, and it was easy to take shelter behind his broad back. If he didn't look up, he could forget where he was.

Until Seb came to an abrupt halt and thrust the magazine page in his face. "Which one is it? They all look the same to me."

"Hmm? Oh, I don't know. Let me look." Dex studied the page and compared it to the racks of weird-looking bags in front of him. Seb was right: they all looked the same, but he kept searching, and eventually his gaze fell on a bag that looked at least similar to the one on the page. "That one?"

"Good enough for me." Seb grabbed the bag without looking at the price, though his eyes did widen slightly when the girl by the till held out her hand. He paid with a card—a concept that boggled Dex's mind—and then all but dragged Dex out of the shop. "Let's get some lunch. I'm starving."

"Already? You just ate."

"Bite me."

Later. And so it went on. Seb bought hot doughnuts from a cart by a bus stop, and they ate them between torturous ordeals in big, horrible shops. Dex didn't want to spend the money in his pocket, but Seb was persuasive. The argument "if you don't buy it, I'll buy it for you" worked for a while, and before Dex knew it, he'd spent fifty quid on new clothes: a coat, some jeans, and some soft trousers to sleep in.

He reached his limit outside the umpteenth shop and dug his feet into the pavement. "No more."

Seb smiled, like he'd expected the mutiny sooner. "No more shopping? Or you want to go home?"

Dex considered his answer. Seb's warm flat was heaven on earth, but walking through London hand in hand felt wonderful, and he wasn't ready to give it up just yet. "No more shopping."

Seb chuckled, the sound deep and mellow and beautifully resonant. "Okay. You gave me less trouble than I expected, so I'll let you off. Have you ever seen Big Ben?"

"Who's that?"

"It's not a person, Dex. It's a landmark. A clock, to be exact. It's by the London Eye. Have you ever seen that?"

"Nope."

Seb hustled him back to the Underground, and ten minutes later, they emerged aboveground at Westminster Tube Station. The clock tower was easy to spot, and, after Seb had positioned them, so was the giant Ferris wheel behind it. The wheel reminded Dex of the summers he'd spent working on fairgrounds before Braden had pulled him into hooking full time. As a child, he'd loved the bright colours of the rides, stalls, and circus tents, but as he'd gotten older, Braden's murky underworld had marred any happy memories he might've had.

"My dad proposed to my mum right over there, way back in '79."

Dex followed Seb's gaze across the street, bustling and brightly lit, ready for the New Year celebrations. "Where?"

"By that bench. It was the first time my mum had ever left Cornwall. By the time they got back, she couldn't wait to do it all over again."

"Is that why your parents live in Spain?"

Seb shifted to stand behind him, encircling him in his strong arms. "Probably. Think they got fed up with the grey English summers. It's a bit of a piss take when the beach is right there all the time, you know?"

Not really, but it didn't matter. All that mattered was the sensation of Seb pressed against him, and the light, sweet kiss that stayed with him long after it was over.

DEX'S BACK hit the thick grey door with a dull thud. Then Seb was on him, kissing his lips, his jaw, his neck, and tugging his hair to grant him better access.

Dex tilted his head, eyes rolling as the scruff on Seb's face scraped his sensitive skin. They'd been inside Seb's flat only moments before the simmering current between them exploded, and he was already lost. He clutched at Seb's clothes, wanting them gone but lacking the coherency to voice it or remove them himself.

He growled his frustration. Seb pulled him from the door and lifted him clean off the floor. "Come to bed?"

"It's six o'clock."

"So? Who's going to know?"

He had a point. Seb said people went out on New Year's Eve if they weren't working, but they had no plans. No plans except this... each other.

It was a while before they fell naked onto Seb's bed—the spiral staircase tricky to navigate while fused to another man—but upstairs, all bets were off. Dex yielded easily beneath Seb, revelling under his solid weight pinning him to the bed. Seb was going to fuck him, he could feel it, and he couldn't wait.

Bare skin, bare skin. I love his skin. Dex slid his hands over Seb's nude back, gliding over the smooth skin and digging his fingers into the grooves of muscle. Seb thrust his hips in response and drove their cocks together. The friction roared through Dex and he moaned... moaned long and low and threw his head back, arching, stretching, feeling the tendons in his neck strain under his overheated skin.

"Please."

Seb thrust again. "Please what? What do you want?"

"You...." Dex jerked, friction, pleasure and utter madness consuming every fibber of him. "You. I... I want you."

Seb stared at him, and something changed in the stormy blue swirls of his eyes. "Say it again. Say it again and you can have anything you want."

"I want you."

The three simple words seemed to wash over Seb, changing him, easing an uncertainty in his gaze Dex had never realised was there.

Seb kissed Dex like he was his most precious thing, and then he fumbled for a condom and pushed inside Dex, slipping into his body in a slow, patient slide. Dex gasped, and for the first time ever with Seb, a yelp of discomfort escaped him. The pain hit him like an old friend. Seb was wide and long, and it seemed a lifetime since anything larger than a gentle finger had breached him this way.

Dex closed his eyes, feeling the burn spread through him like lava, seeping into his bones and rushing to the tips of his fingers and toes. Seb shifted, giving him room to breathe and make himself comfortable, and Dex wanted to cry. The way Seb let him move... let him take from him as much as he gave... he'd dreamed of this.

Seb coaxed his eyes open with a soft caress of his cheek. "All right? Tell me what you need."

Dex could hardly hear him over the stampeding thud of his heart. He flexed his hips, shuddering at the lightning bolt of pleasure. "I...."

What? What did he need? It wasn't a question he'd ever been asked before, and in his mind, he'd always pictured the moment they came together again as hard and fast, his face mashed into the mattress as Seb pounded him from behind. That fantasy had its merits, but it wasn't what he craved.

Seb rolled his hips, moving his cock in and out in a long, slow motion. Dex moaned, and the pain morphed from a fiery sting to a bright spark of pure pleasure. "Again. Do it again."

He arched his back, thrusting his hips to take Seb deeper, and Seb responded, fucking him slowly… sweetly, until the push and pull of his cock was so perfect Dex could feel nothing else.

CHAPTER TWENTY-ONE

THE BODY beside Dex shifted, stealing away its precious warmth. Dex protested, still mostly asleep, and followed the heat, seeking out its soothing, addictive comfort.

He found it in the shape of curved flesh dusted with a fine layer of hair that tickled his face. He flinched, wrinkling his nose.

Seb chuckled. "Let me up, Dex. I need to get ready for work."

"No." Dex burrowed deeper. "You're warm."

"What's that?" Seb rolled them over, covered Dex with his body and pressed his ear to his cheek. "I can't understand you when you mutter like that."

That's the point. To stop the gorjers understanding. Dex didn't know he was doing it half the time. He wriggled out from beneath Seb and fastened his arm around his middle, tugging him closer, throwing the duvet back over him and burying his face in his chest. "Too early."

"Only because you're a sloth."

"A what?"

"A lazy arse. Let me up."

Dex scowled. Seb often made fun of him for his reluctance to leave the big, soft, Seb-smelling bed, especially when Seb was in it too. He also found great amusement in Dex's newfound love of using him as a pillow.

"Face it, mate. You just want a bloody cuddle."

Sad, but true. "Do we have to get up?"

Seb nuzzled Dex's hair, inhaling him in much the same way Dex did the pillows when Seb wasn't looking. "Unless you give me a reason to stay put."

Dex lifted his head. They were both naked. Seb had his eyes closed, but his smirk was wide, and trapped beneath Dex's thigh, his dick was thick and hard. Cautiously, Dex raised himself to lie over Seb, their bodies pressed together in every way possible. They'd had sex a lot since the first time—at least once every day, sometimes more—and Seb seemed to like it when he lay on top of him. "What kind of reason?"

"This'll do."

Seb wrapped his arms around him. In return, Dex studied him. His eyes remained closed, and he seemed pretty relaxed for someone desperate to get out of bed. Maybe it was a ploy, a ploy to get him to… to get him to what? Dex had no idea. He thought back to a few days before, when Seb had passed him a box of ingredients with no recipe or instructions.

"Follow your instincts. Do what feels right."

For Dex, it seemed what felt right was often the first thing that came into his head. He sucked Seb's nipple into his mouth, then bit down, remembering the sensation of Seb's teeth grazing his own chest.

Seb tensed, arched a little from the mattress, and inhaled a shaky breath. Encouraged, Dex kissed a path to Seb's other nipple, instinctively bearing down on the hard cock grinding beneath him. This time, Seb groaned and shuddered like a ghost had walked over his grave.

"All right, all right. Fuck work. I'm staying right here."

Dex looked up and grinned, but he was far from done, and he took his time exploring Seb's chest like he'd never seen or touched it before. Seb squirmed beneath him, letting him have his way awhile before he lost patience and yanked him up the bed. He reached behind him into the canny stash between the mattress and the wall and tossed a tube of lube and condom onto his chest.

"I'm all yours."

Dex considered what it would be like to roll the condom onto himself and slide into Seb's body. Seb had hinted more than once it was something he'd like, but Dex dismissed the thought, too caught up in the sensation of Seb's cock pressing against him... too far gone to contemplate anything but that dick pushing inside him and consuming his soul.

He started to climb off Seb and roll onto his back. Seb stilled him. "Try it like this."

Seb slid a finger into Dex, and then another, stretching him out, preparing him for his cock in a way that put Dex right on the edge before they'd even gotten started. Dex bit his lip, fighting for control, and when he could take no more, he pulled off and took hold of Seb's dick.

He eased himself down, steadying himself with his hands on Seb's chest, letting the heat and pressure of being filled rush through him. His thighs touched Seb's hips. Seb rubbed Dex's legs and kissed the tips of his fingers.

"That's it. Take it slow."

Dex watched his finger disappear into the sweet warmth of Seb's mouth. He wanted to rock his hips so slowly Seb's eyes rolled into the back of his head, but the sensation of Seb's tongue dancing on his finger put paid to that.

His body moved of its own accord, falling into the primal rhythm that flowed so easily between him and Seb. Up, down, and around. Up, down, and around. It became a mantra in his head, an unrelenting chant that seeped into his limbs and took over where his brain failed.

Fucking Seb like this, riding him... it felt amazing, and until Seb gripped his wrist and guided his hand to his own cock, he pretty much forgot all about it.

Pleasuring himself was a new experience too, but he was a quick learner. He pumped his fist, tightening and twisting, watching his dick swell and seep. The first real strains of release shuddered through him. He gasped, and the steady pace of his hips faltered. Seb took over, holding him still and thrusting up into him again and again until they came within moments of each other. Dex first... always Dex first.

Dex fell, exhausted, on Seb. Seb squeezed him tight and mashed their sticky bodies together. "Fuck, fuck, fuck. That was amazing, and we're so fucking late."

Dex laughed, sprawled in Seb's arms, content, and prepared to stay there forever. "That's a lot of fucks."

"Yeah, but you can never have enough when it's as good as this."

DEX STARED at Rick in muted horror, unsure he'd heard right. "You want me to work on the grill?"

"Aye, lad." Rick hardly spared him a glance from the order pad he was scrutinizing. Dex could just about decipher the word "fruit" at the top of the page, but any sense of achievement was marred by a growing wave of panic. "You've been with Seb a month now. It's a new year, and time to move on. Moses will look after you."

"Not Damon?"

"Damon's a shite teacher. You'll learn more with Moses."

Rick said no more. Dex took his leave and trudged to the dessert counter to retrieve his hat and cloth. Seb met his gaze with an encouraging smile, but it wasn't enough to dampen the raw, painful fear of being separated from him. Dex was more comfortable in the volatile kitchen than he could quite believe, but there was no denying he spent much of his time hiding behind Seb and his gentle, broad shoulders.

Grill chef Moses was a different creature altogether. Bigger than Seb, he had a deep, gruff voice and a fiery temper that sent even the feistiest waitress running back to the bar. In his own, silent way, Dex was terrified.

He approached the grill with a heavy heart, feeling the heat of it hit him even this early in the morning. The heavy extractor fans whirred above his head, and the air was thick with the scent of smoky meat.

Moses regarded him with curious eyes. "The prodigal baker coming over to the dark side, eh? Right, get your board out. Let's get started."

Grill prep was less involved than dessert prep, and Dex was well versed in stocking the deep counter drawers with the various cuts of meat, game, and poultry. The fish was more of a challenge. Dex could fillet a mackerel with his eyes closed, but he spent most of his morning staring at squid and wondering if he'd been dropped into another world. Bloody things looked and felt like cold, slimy jizz.

Still, at least he didn't annoy Moses. The hardheaded chef was a man of few words, and it seemed the less he said, the better his mood.

Lunchtime service started with a bang. Four tickets came through at once, and Moses, in contrast to Seb's easy banter, bellowed his orders in Dex's ear.

Dex jumped a mile. Moses paid him no heed and passed him a ticket. "Put two sirloins, a fillet, and a burger on. I'll show you how to test them when they've got a bit of colour on them."

"Yes, chef." Dex slapped the meat on the grill, flinching as the fat sizzled and popped. He pressed it down with a heavy pair of tongs, waiting for the grill lines to take hold.

Moses appeared at his shoulder. "Let's have a look. Right, see this sirloin? Give it a poke. It feels like a sponge, eh? That means it's blue. Keep poking it, and tell me when you think it's changed."

Dex pressed his finger into the steak again and again, until finally, he felt the meat tighten. "Now. It feels harder."

"That's right." Moses seemed pleased. "It's rare now. It'll be medium rare in a few more minutes, and then medium. If it feels like a brick, it's medium well. We don't serve well-done steak here, so don't even ask about that."

And so the lesson went on, and the day disappeared with it. Moses wasn't quite the terrifying demon Dex had feared he would be, but the relentless heat of the grill proved hotter than he'd ever imagined. The atmosphere was different too: blunt, brutal, and uncompromising. At the height of a busy service, there was nowhere to hide and no time to be afraid. No amount of prep could save a chef from the weight of fifteen steaks on the grill.

At the end of his shift, Dex cleaned the section, feeling battered and bruised, but in a good way. It reminded him of being fucked by Seb—the sensation of being thoroughly used combined with total and utter exhaustion.

He glanced at the clock. By his reckoning, it was a little after ten. He frowned. That couldn't be right. Most nights, it was past eleven by the time he washed down the countertops. He looked over at Seb, saw he was still busy plating up orders, and it dawned on him that this was how it went on the grill. Service came in a deep, intense blur, but it was over before the dessert counter had really begun. He was done for the day, but Seb had just gotten started.

Moses dismissed him, and it seemed only natural to drift over to Seb and help him, but Seb shooed him away.

"No chance. You look done in. Besides, I need to get used to doing this shit on my own again. Go home. I'll ring you when I'm done."

"Home?"

Seb rolled his eyes. "Okay, my place, the flat, whatever. I put a spare key in your locker upstairs. Think you can remember the code?"

Sneaky git. "Four-three-eight-zero."

"That's it." Seb winked and turned away to rescue a crème brûlée from under the grill. "Just don't fall asleep, okay? I've got something to tell you."

Dex was curious, but Seb was too busy to elaborate, so he left him to it, pulled his new hat over his head, and walked… *home* alone. On the way, he braved the corner shop and bought Seb some beer and bacon for breakfast the next morning. He was still getting used to pottering around Seb's kitchen. Most times, he found himself waiting for the bogeyman to jump out behind him, to wake him up and prove that his happy bubble with Seb was indeed a dream, but it hadn't happened yet.

A warm glow buzzed through his veins as he walked along. The day had started with the best sex he'd ever had—apart from the day before, and the day before that—and would likely end the same way. The bit in between hadn't been half-bad either. The grill was terrifying, but as Dex drifted along the pavement, lost in his thoughts, he couldn't help but feel excited. For the first time in his life, he felt constructive... productive, like his existence had purpose, and, aside from the sensation of Seb's arms sliding around his waist, it was the best feeling in the world.

The streets of Dalston faded to a lively roar. A car slowed to a crawl beside him, but he didn't look up. The Turkish youths in the area had a habit of cruising the curbs and shouting into the brightly lit barbershops.

Dex didn't take much notice until the passenger door opened in his face and sent him sprawling to his knees.

"*Grālt'a*, boyo. Missed me?"

CHAPTER TWENTY-TWO

DEX LAY still and listened to the noises. Some sounds were scary—like the rumble of a vehicle or the slam of a door—but others were soothing. His head throbbed and he could taste dried blood on his lips, but the call of a kestrel somewhere high in the sky was nice. Male kestrels had blue wings. Dex liked blue things.

He opened his eyes and looked around. His "cell" was pitch-black and windowless. He figured he was tied up in the back of Mikey's van somewhere on a site or a disused piece of farmland. It wouldn't be the first time.

"Grālt'a, boyo."

The innocuous greeting echoed in his aching head, and the rough Shelta chilled his blood even now... long after rough hands had pulled him from the pavement and banged his head against the door of Mikey's van until he no longer cared if they killed him right there on the street. He'd lost the hat Seb gave him too, and despite the pain in his battered body, he felt the loss like a knife to his chest.

Seb. It felt like a lifetime since Dex had said good-bye to him, but he had no real idea how long it had really been. In the darkness of wherever he was confined, he couldn't tell if it was night or day, let alone how much time had lapsed since he'd lost consciousness and come to. It could've been hours, or even days.

How long would Seb wait for him before he gave up and went back to a life uncomplicated by an illiterate whore in his bed?

The thought tortured Dex as he drifted in that cold, barren place between wakefulness and oblivion, and it was only the jangly rumble of an approaching vehicle that roused him sometime later. Voices came next. They seemed magnified by the time they reached him, and fear stabbed at his heart, but simmering beneath was the paradoxical comfort that he wasn't alone. Dex didn't like being alone, not anymore.

The van door cranked open and flooded the inside with a flash of painful white light. *So it's daylight, then.* Dex screwed his eyes shut and tried to turn away, but the chains binding him held him in place.

A rough hand grasped his chin. *Mikey.* "Come on, kid. Time to face the music."

Dex swallowed thickly and tried to detach his tongue from the roof of his mouth. "Are we going back to the site?"

Mikey snorted and spat onto the muddy ground. "There is no site. The gorjers shut it down. This is it... all Braden's got left, and you're his only entertainment. Be quiet and do as you're told, and maybe he'll kill you quickly."

It was a phrase Dex had heard before, and in the past it had had little effect on him. *Kill me. I don't care.* But he cared now... cared so much that the threat of his inevitable execution made his empty stomach lurch. He'd already been sick, several times over, but he retched anyway.

Mikey unchained him and hurled him from the van like a sack of flour. Dex hit the frosted ground with a bone-jarring thump. Mikey kicked him. "Walk."

Dex walked, head down, and stumbled along the icy dirt until they reached an outbuilding. Mikey shoved him inside and chained him to a low-hanging wooden beam. Then he tapped Dex's face with his fist and left him alone to await his fate.

He didn't have to wait long. Braden appeared just as he lost the last remnants of sensation in his tightly bound hands.

"Well, well, well. Not so quick on your feet now, eh?"

Braden yanked Dex's head up and forced him to meet his bloodshot stare. Dex blinked and slipped into his well-versed role of a muted, submissive idiot. He knew better than to react.

He watched through clouded eyes as Braden paced in front of him. He knew Braden's face and form almost better than he knew his own—the hulking frame that disguised a subtle limp, the ruddy skin, calloused fingers, and huge, powerful hands. Hands that had used and abused Dex for years. He wondered how he'd found him. Of all places, Dalston wasn't the most obvious to look.

On cue, Braden came to a stop in front of him. "We saw you with your boy toy in the city. Don't think I won't find out who he is. Is that why you stayed away so long? Busy fucking your gorjer lover, eh?"

"He's not mine." Dex thought quickly. "He was a john."

Braden's expression hardened and morphed from one of petty revenge to fury. Denting Braden's pride was one thing, but earning money without giving him his cut? There was no worse crime, and Dex knew he would be punished.

He expected the blow to his face. He lurched sideways with the force of it and felt the blood burst through his already cracked lips. It hurt like hell, but he felt detached from it, like he was floating above and looking down upon himself. Like a dream? No, and not even a nightmare. It just... was.

Braden hit him again and again, punched and backhanded him. Dex ignored it all until Braden's knee came up and pounded him in the stomach.

Dex groaned a choking, inhuman groan. His breath left his body. His bones rattled and his teeth shook. He coughed and spluttered and ripped his throat raw.

Braden laughed. "Yeah. Now you feel me, boyo. Think you can hide from me? After all I've done for you? Let's see if you remember how to behave." Dex abruptly found himself facing the wall behind him, his face mashed into the cold stone. Braden ripped his T-shirt away and whistled. "Someone's been feeding you up. Not sure I like you as much without the bones. Let's see what the others think."

Braden called out, and heavy footsteps answered him. Behind Dex, the outbuilding filled with voices—some he recognized and some he didn't. Or maybe he didn't recognize any of them. Maybe the voices of animals about to go feral all sounded the same.

Someone pulled on his hair, clipped his ear, and thumped his ribs. Dex closed his eyes, sure he felt the bones crack, and then the rest of the blows washed over him, merging together and becoming nothing more than an undefined haze of bruising pain. The accompanying, muttered words stood out more.

"Whore."

"Slag."

"Bitch."

"You little bag of shit."

Something inside Dex snapped. Anger and resentment raced through him, swelling his veins and filling his soul with a self-respect he'd never known before. He wasn't a bag of shit, and he didn't belong to anyone, not Seb, not Braden and his motley gang of thugs.

Fuck. You.

Rebellion surged through him, and for a moment, it felt wonderful. He fought his chains and relished the bite of them against his tender flesh. He kicked out with his legs, catching someone… maybe Braden… with his foot. Pride surged through him. He wasn't a bag of shit, or if he was, he was his own bag of shit.

Kill me if you want, but you'll never own me again.

Dex spat blood from the corner of his mouth. He ran his tongue over his teeth. Somehow, they were all still there. Hysterical laughter bubbled in his chest. It was the fourth day he'd been strung up in the barn—maybe the fifth; he'd lost the will to count —and it seemed his value as communal entertainment had finally waned. Only Braden remained, and he regarded Dex now through beady eyes. He'd yet to use the crowbar swinging at his side, but the threat was clear. Braden stopped in front of him. He was sweating, which struck Dex as odd. Stripped to his waist, his jeans so stained with blood and mud they looked like biker leathers, Dex was cold to the bone, and through the cracked window of the deserted outbuilding, he could see a thin layer of snow dusted the ground.

"Who did you tell?"

Dex jerked his head up, unaware he'd slumped forward and closed his eyes. "Tell what?"

"What you saw." Braden stepped closer and jammed the metal bar into Dex's ribs. "You've never run from me before. Who told you to run?"

"No one."

"Liar." Braden twisted the bar, gouging a hole in Dex's skin to match the other cuts and scrapes. "Police are looking for me. They know what I did. Who told them, boyo, eh? Who told them?"

"I… don't know."

Braden hit him. The world went black for a while, and he was alone when he came round. At least he thought he was, until someone unchained him and he fell to the ground in a heap.

Mikey hauled him to his feet. "Get up."

"Why?" Arguing was futile and dangerous, but after hours bound with his arms above his head, curling up on the ground felt like heaven.

Mikey glanced at him, eyebrow raised. "Because I said so. Now get the fuck up."

Dex got up and took a quick inventory of his battered body. His legs were bruised but sound. His arms too. His torso hurt the most—his chest and his ribs. It hurt to breathe. He wished he could stop.

He stumbled. Mikey took his arm and led him out of the barn. The daylight hurt his eyes, but he wasn't in it for long. Mikey towed him across a yard and shoved him inside the deserted farmhouse. A fire burned in a dilapidated room that had once been a kitchen.

To Dex's surprise, Mikey pushed him to the floor close enough so he could feel its precious heat. "Sit there and shut up."

Dex hugged his knees to his chest and wrapped his arms around himself. He felt dazed and detached, but a part of him was vaguely aware Mikey's behaviour was more than a little odd.

The feeling increased when Mikey tossed a Mars bar his way. Hunger overcame him. He tore the wrapper and inhaled the chocolate in two choking bites. Mikey knelt in front of him and held a bottle of water to his mouth. He tapped a finger to his lips as he pulled away, then drew an imaginary blade across his throat.

A word about this and I'll kill you.

Dex gulped at the water, knowing it could be days before he got any more. His greed proved his undoing. He choked and it came out of his nose. Mikey took the water away, like he'd come to his senses, and cuffed him. The blow was halfhearted. Seemed more for show than anything else, but Dex felt it like a bat to the head.

"We've been looking for you for months." Dex opened his watery eyes. Mikey stood by the open door, blowing cigarette smoke into the chilly air. "We thought another gang had picked you up, put you to work. Didn't think you had it in you to go it alone."

Dex considered his words. Braden had swallowed his assertion that Seb was a nameless john. He wanted to keep it that way, so Seb could forget he ever existed. "How did you find me?"

"By accident. Wasn't even looking for you. Me and Shane was scoutin' a job, and there you were, snoggin' your trick by that jock-off clock."

Big Ben. Seb had kissed Dex under the stars and stared at him like he was the most precious thing in the world. The knowledge that Mikey and his mates had unwittingly intruded on that made Dex want to puke again.

"The job was a crock of shite too." Mikey leaned on the doorpost and looked up at the sky. "Way out of Braden's league, and that's his bloody problem. Bastard's going to take us all down with him."

Dex laid his cheek on his bent knees. Mikey's voice was far away, and he felt sleepy. He didn't care about Mikey, or Braden, or their failed attempt to become big-time gangsters. He just wanted to sleep.

"Someone's talking to the coppers." Suddenly, Mikey was beside him again. "Braden thinks it's you, but I know it's not. You're just a kid. You don't know enough to stir up the shite that's gone down. You don't know the bloody half of it, and I'll tell you one thing for nothing, kid. I'm not going down for no one, least of all that cunt."

Mikey took hold of Dex's chin. Dex flinched and confusion scattered his thoughts. Mikey was Braden's right-hand man, stoic and loyal, and he'd never once shown a hint of dissent. And one of their own talking to the police? To the gorjers? No. It would never happen. Traveller silence was sacred. They didn't talk to outsiders.

A vehicle rumbled into the muddy yard. Dex closed his eyes, knowing it was Braden. Mikey released him and stepped away. He called a terse greeting through the open door. Braden's reply was gruff, and for a moment, Dex wondered if Mikey would make his move. Express his discontent and strike out. Kill Braden, or disable him. Perhaps there'd even be a moment for Dex to slip away. He wasn't bound, and his legs still worked. He could run.

I can run.

But nothing happened. Mikey said no more and left the house, abandoning him to Braden's ill will and deepening temper. Chains, leather belts, and iron bars. Dex bore it all in silence until his wrist bone broke with an audible snap.

CHAPTER TWENTY-THREE

DEX CURLED up in the pitch-black of the van. His throat was raw from screaming and his broken arm hung limp at his side, but he felt no pain. Not anymore. Pain was old news, almost a distant memory, and instead, he felt nothing. Nothing at all. He heard voices from time to time, and tried to worry that they might've been coming for him, but he didn't care. Not anymore. His perspective had gone and he was floating. Reality and his own imagination blurred together, and though he knew he was alone in the back of the van, if he squeezed his eyes shut, he found himself back in the barn... back with Braden. The snap of his wrist echoed in his head, and he remembered Braden untying him and letting him fall to the ground. Blood had flowed back into Dex's uninjured arm, and his eyes had rolled with the pleasure of it.

Braden had seen his reaction and struck him with a length of hose. "You sick little whore."

Yeah. Maybe Braden was right.

Dex licked his cracked lips. He was thirsty. In between Braden's increasingly deranged interrogations, Mikey had been slipping him water and the occasional scrap of food, but it had been a while... a few days, maybe? He'd lost track, but he hadn't seen Mikey in quite some time. Somewhere in the back of Dex's mind, he was aware it had been a long while since he'd seen *anyone*, that even his torture sessions had petered out, but he couldn't be sure. He was distracted. The hunger didn't bother him —it was like an old friend—but the thirst... God, the thirst. Slowly and surely, it was driving him mad.

Dex closed his eyes. Sounds echoed around the disused farm-land, and he tried to gauge the time. The voices and vehicles meant nothing—Braden came for him at all hours—but Dex recognized the birdcalls. They were owls, and the owls only came out at night. Dex strained his ears and heard foxes too, the call of the vixens to their mates. The gravelly screams took him back to London and the first time he'd seen an urban fox scavenging in the bins of the restaurant. He'd watched the young fox, a cub, really, crunch through discarded meat bones for ages before Seb came to get him, and he'd felt a strange and ancient affinity with the wild, resourceful creature. Were it not for hunting and technol-ogy, foxes would outlast them all.

"You like animals, don't you?"

Seb's voice washed over Dex, warming him from the inside out like the shot of amber whiskey Rick had passed him on Christmas Day.

No. Don't think of him. It's too late. He's gone.

Dex pushed Seb from his mind, but the lull was brief, because in a place where darkness felt like it would last forever, the lure of his memory proved too tempting to resist. Even imagined, fantasy Seb was a balm to his wounds.

"You look like a dormouse burrowed up in there."

Dex smiled, and the haze overcame him. He let his eyelids fall closed and drifted to a place where Seb's voice was real, his hands strong and warm and the only hands in the world....

"It's just a bedroom, Dex. See for yourself." Seb held out his hand, amused, his grin wide and welcoming.

Dex stared at the spiral staircase. It was harsh and metallic, like the rest of the converted warehouse, and he couldn't imagine it leading anywhere nice. And why did Seb want him to go up there? Dex's experi-ences with stairs had never been good. Though his time with Seb had proved an exception to every rule, Dex always seemed to end up some-

where dark and unpleasant when he went up or down a set of stairs he didn't trust. "Why is your bedroom up there?"

"Why not?" Seb shrugged and stepped closer. He caught Dex's hand before he could protest. "Bedrooms are upstairs in houses, right? And they make all these conversions weird when they convert them, so they can pack us in like sardines."

Dex touched the banister. It was smooth and flawless, like the big high slide in the play park at Kilkenny Castle—the play park he and his cousins had used to break into in the dead of night before his da had sent him away.

"I'm not expecting you to sleep with me, Dex. I just want you to know you can... if you want to."

"Do you want me to?" Dex took his hand from the banister and turned away from the shiny metal steps. Seb was closer than he'd thought, and it seemed natural to lean against him.

Seb held him a moment, then released him and stepped away. "I do, but more than that, I want you to be comfortable. Maybe we could switch some nights. You take the bed. I'll sleep on the couch."

"I don't want to sleep in your bed without you."

Seb raised an eyebrow but said nothing, and the silence crept over Dex like a wave. He put a foot on the bottom step. Nothing bad happened. No one came rushing down or shoved him to his knees. Seb didn't suddenly morph into a raging monster.

Behind him, Seb laughed. "Do you want me to go first?"

It was a ridiculous concession, but one that turned out to be valid. Seb preceded him up the stairs, and after that, it seemed easy to follow him....

"Are you trying to tell me I'm fat?"

Dex watched Seb amble around the room and get himself ready for bed. "Eh?"

Seb gestured at Dex and the way he was lying, curled up at the top of the mattress with his head barely on the pillow. "You can have more space than that, mate."

Dex chewed the inside of his mouth and uncurled his legs. The bed was huge, and he felt lost, like he didn't know how to behave. Silly, really, considering he'd shared a bed with Seb before.

He muffled his sigh with a cough. Things had seemed different back then. He'd climbed into Seb's bed that night believing he'd never see him again, and somehow, it had seemed easier that way. Now... this was something Seb wanted him to do every night, and Dex simply didn't know how.

Seb slid into the bed. He rolled onto his side and fiddled with the duvet until it was covering them both to his liking. Dex watched him, curious. The duvet was thick and white... like a marshmallow, but it felt as light as air.

Weird.

Seb turned out the light. Darkness swallowed him, and for a long moment, he was invisible. Dex blinked and scooted across the bed like a lizard. He found Seb's chest and clung to him like he'd been gone for a year.

"I could get used to this." Seb chuckled softly and kissed Dex's hair. He wrapped him in an embrace that felt like the sun on an early summer morning. "Feels right."

Dex pressed closer, shoved his head under Seb's arm. Yeah, it felt right, but it felt like a dream, and the trouble with dreams was he always woke up.

VOICES ROUSED Dex from his catatonic doze. He listened, unmoving, for a moment, waiting for the familiar roar of Braden or Mikey's sardonic grumble, but the shouts echoing around the deserted farmland were new. New and *loud*. For the first time in days, fear crept into Dex's hazily detached, Seb-filled world. Pain flared, and he shivered. He hadn't noticed the cold for a while, but he was still shirtless and dressed only in his dirty jeans.

The voices got louder and grew in number. Dex counted two, four, six before he lost track. He curled his battered body tighter, cradling his wrist, and tried to make himself as small as possible.

Braden was out there somewhere, and he'd come for him for sure. There was nothing Braden liked more than an audience.

The ground beneath the van rumbled. A vehicle passed by, its engine deep and low, like a lorry or a pickup truck. Dex held his breath, as if it would stop whoever was out there from wrenching open the van door.

An earsplitting crack pierced the air. *Gunfire*. A few months ago, he'd have thought it the sound of a backfiring car, but he knew better now. Cora's deadened eyes flashed into his mind and terror clawed at him.

Outside, all hell broke loose. Shouting, pounding footsteps, and barking dogs. More vehicles came. Someone screamed, yelled out in pain like an animal caught in a trap.

The wail was primal and resonant, and it touched every nerve in Dex's body like a spark to a fuse. He turned his head and vomited bile. What were they going to do? Open the van doors and shoot his bloody head off? A few hours ago, he thought he didn't care, but he did… God, he did. He didn't want to die in the back of a stinking van, illiterate and worthless. He didn't want to die without ever telling Seb he thought he loved him.

Love. Seb. The two words were made for each other. Dex had written them down once, side by side on a paper napkin, just to see if he could. The result was mixed, but the tingling in his chest had remained for days. He hadn't known what it meant at the time, but he knew now.

I love you, Seb. I love you and I want to come home…. I want to come back to the restaurant, learn to read, and let Moses shout at me as much as he wants.

Home. Another word that used to mean nothing, but with Seb, it had come to mean everything. Everything and nothing at all if Dex died right here. Would Seb ever know? Probably not. He'd taken the time to care for Dex on a level Dex hadn't known existed, but in reality, Seb knew nothing about Dex. He didn't even know his name.

He doesn't know who I am.

More gunshots whistled through the air. Some were light, like the pop of an air rifle, and sounded far, far away, but others shook the ground, whizzing through Dex's veins like every bullet would surely explode in his brain. He heard cracks, thuds, and shouts. Then periods of silence so long he felt like he'd imagined the noise to begin with. It sounded like a war zone. Perhaps it was. Perhaps Mikey had turned his rambling mutiny into something that mattered.

A bullet pierced the van and lodged in the dented metal by Dex's foot. He stared at it, absently wondering what it would feel like when the end came... when the bullet with his name on it blasted into his body. Would it hurt? Maybe not, if it hit the right place. Perhaps he should cut his losses and climb out of the van. Give himself up and ask them to kill him. For the first time, it occurred to him he'd never checked to see if the doors were locked.

You don't have to do everything I say. Don't move. *It's up to you.* Stay. *You choose.* Down. *Whatever you want.* Quiet.

What do you want, Dex?

Dex bit down on his fist and screamed.

CHAPTER TWENTY-FOUR

"Bloody hell. This one's alive."

The voice was so deep and gentle it could've been Seb. The palm of a large hand came to rest on Dex's forehead, and two fingers touched his neck. Smaller hands grasped his wrist. Someone moaned.

Daylight flooded the van. More voices came, men and women. More men. Dex stared up at them, powerless to act on the terror coursing through him. He was frozen, trapped inside his own body, and unable to stop the new faces from doing with him as they pleased.

He felt himself being lifted from the cold metal floor of the van. Shiny blankets covered him. They felt warm… a sign of his depleted mental state. A hard plastic mask came down on his face. Cold air blasted into his mouth. Dex squirmed and tried to push it away. Big hands held him down, clamping around his snapped wrist, and the world as he knew it went black.

It was a while before he became aware of himself again. He caught flashes as the scenery changed. Blue lights, more daylight, and those strips of blinding fluorescent bulbs you got in corridors. Hands touched him and shook him. Peeled his eyes open and shouted in his face. He was poked and prodded, his body bent this way and that. The experience was painfully familiar, though different from Braden's usual style. Dex's arm hurt so much he threw up on himself, until it didn't and he couldn't feel it at all. He worried Braden had cut it off. The logic made sense. It was broken and useless, like him. What else would he do with it? What else would he do with *him*?

Shoot him. That's what Braden did with horses. Why didn't he shoot him? *Because Braden isn't here.* But where was he? Perhaps he'd been sold. Braden sold his horses from time to time, and he'd threatened to sell Dex before.

Earn your keep, boyo. Or I'll turn you over to a cunt far worse than me.

Dex. Dex. Dex.

Dex rolled over, curling his body inward to avoid the persistent voices calling his name, or maybe to hide from his own madness. Braden didn't call him Dex…. Didn't *know* about Dex, and resistance was futile. Wherever he was, Braden would come for him eventually. Shame, really, because Dex rather liked this weird place where his limbs felt detached and his mind not his own. His last stand? Maybe, but if Braden wanted him, he'd have to come get him.

Sometime later—hours, days, he didn't much care—the incessant voices morphed into a rough hand on Dex's uninjured arm. A gentle shake and a familiar cough. Curiosity eased into Dex's veins, washing away the fear lodged deep in his belly. He opened his eyes. Rick's ruddy face stared back at him.

"All right, lad?"

Dex swallowed. The hospital room had been a blur up until then, but suddenly, it was clear as day, his focus so sharp he saw every line and wrinkle in Rick's face like it was in 3D. Yeah. Like that film Seb took him to see, the one with the liquid spacesuits.

"Dex, you with me?" Rick helped him sit upright and stared at him for a long moment. "You've had us all worried. Jesus, lad. Bernie's been up the wall and tickling the bricks. You all right? Need anything?"

Need? Dex looked around and took in the rumpled bed. Strange clothes covered his body and a weird tube protruded from the back of his hand. His other arm was blue, strapped to his chest, and sheathed in a cast that glimmered with a strange, alienesque sheen.

"Fiberglass," Rick supplied. "It was too bad for a plaster cast."

Dex frowned, wondering if he'd been dropped into another world. His gaze fell on a full bottle of orange squash. His mouth watered. "Whose is that?"

"Yours." Rick proffered a foil-wrapped parcel Dex hadn't noticed. "They said you can eat today too. Seb made you some flapjacks. Want some?"

Seb's here. "Where is he? Where's Seb?"

"I sent him to get you some clothes before he punched a copper. He'll be back soon."

Dex eyed the foil-wrapped package Rick had in his hands. It was messy and loose, like the parcels of fudge Seb used to sell in Padstow. *Seb's shit at wrapping things up.*

"Have some, son. He made it for you."

Despite Seb's poor attempt at wrapping, Dex couldn't make his shaky hand work enough to open the parcel. Rick helped him, and then he held a plastic cup of orange squash to his lips. Dex drank greedily and spilled half of it down his front. Rick chuckled, though the sound was hollow, and passed him a small square of sticky flapjack.

Dex shoved it in his mouth, suddenly so hungry he could bite his own arm off—his good one, at least. He ate another, and another before Rick took them away.

"Easy now. Little and often, they said. Have some more in a bit."

Dex hugged his knees to his chest with his good arm, breathless from the effort of stuffing his face. "I'm hungry."

"Not surprised. Half-starved you were when them coppers found you. You can have some more in a bit, I promise. Just don't want you upchucking it all over my boots."

Dex chewed on his lip. That was the second time Rick had mentioned the police—the enemy, in Dex's world. "Where did they find me?"

"Some farm in the west country. Not sure where. They're not telling us much."

"Who isn't?"

"The coppers—"

The curtain around the bed drew back. A woman doctor with long braids smiled at him. "Good to see you back on your feet, Mr Sweeney."

Dex hadn't heard his family name for so long it took a moment to realise she was talking to him. Then he just about fell off the bed. How did the gorjer doctor know his name? *No one* knew his name. Braden had said he didn't need one, and he'd been without it so long he barely knew it himself.

The doctor came closer and set a big brown envelope on the bedside cabinet. "How are you feeling? You were quite dehydrated when you arrived, but we've given you fluids for that." The doctor took in the spilled squash and flapjack crumbs. "I see you've managed to eat something. That's good."

The doctor looked at him expectantly, but Dex didn't know what to say. Only knew what he felt. "Can I leave?"

"Not quite yet. Another doctor needs to check your wrist, and we have some other tests to do." The doctor glanced over his head at Rick, who looked like he wished the ground would swallow him up. "Would you mind stepping outside a moment?"

"Tests?" Dex reached out for Rick as he stood to go. He didn't want Rick, he wanted Seb, but he couldn't be alone. What if Braden came back? He wouldn't be far away. He was *never* far away. "What kind of tests?"

The doctor put her pen down, lining it up next to her big fat envelope with unnecessary care. "The police are concerned you may have been sexually assaulted. We'd like to do an internal examination to check for injuries. Are you okay with that?"

Internal.... Dex ripped his hand from Rick's arm like he'd been burned, and Rick disappeared, the curtain flapping in his wake like a ghost. Panic rose in Dex's chest. Rick had known what the doctor meant before she spelled it out. Rick *knew*... knew he was a whore, and if Rick knew, then Seb… fuck. Was that why he wasn't here?

"No."

The doctor raised an eyebrow. "No, what?"

"I don't want you to look at me."

"Mr Sweeney—"

"*No.* They didn't fuck me."

And it was true. This time, at least. Dex was battered and bruised, but Braden hadn't fucked him. No one had fucked him since Seb.

Seb, Seb, Seb. Where was he?

The doctor said no more. A nurse joined her, and together, they poked and prodded him, but thankfully, their attention remained on the outside of his body. Dex did his best to ignore them until the nurse pulled the tube from the back of his hand. Blood seeped out of the hole. The nurse covered it with a plaster, but his stomach clenched and he wanted to hurl the precious food he'd stuffed into his belly.

The nurse smiled and passed him some more squash with her spare hand. "Have a drink. It'll pass."

Dex drank, grateful for the distraction. Sensation had filtered back into his casted wrist, and the throbbing ache was beginning to radiate up his arm and into his whole body. He felt tired too, like he could sleep for a week and still be exhausted.

His head dropped lower and lower until determined footsteps caught his attention. He snapped upright, alert. Two suited men appeared around the curtain, and Dex shrank back, scooting up the bed until his back was against the small wooden cabinet. The men were coppers. They had to be. Only coppers looked at him the way they were now.

The doctor rounded the bed and effectively put herself between Dex and the men. "Can this wait? He hasn't seen his partner yet."

The taller of the two men shook his head. "We need his statement. Mr Wright gave us his clothes. We'll step outside while he gets changed."

The doctor protested, the nurse too, but the men paid them no heed. A bundle of clothes was exchanged, and the nurse approached Dex with what she probably thought was a reassuring smile. "They just want to ask you some questions. Don't worry. You're safe here. No one's going to hurt you."

"TELL US again. How long have you been in England?"

Really? Again? Dex traced his fingertip down the strange cast on his arm. It felt light and thin, like plastic, but if he knocked it with his knuckle, it sounded like steel. "A long time."

"How long?"

"Dunno."

"And you spent all that time with Braden McCulloch?"

Dex hummed, turning his attention to the dented can of Tizer the detectives had tried to bribe him with. The conversation was going round on a loop, but it wasn't without merit. So far, he'd learned he'd been in the Bristol hospital for nearly a week.

Bristol. Where the hell is that?

"You said your father sent you to work for Mr McCulloch when you were very young. Declan, you do realise you were sold… trafficked as a slave, don't you?"

Dex shrugged. *If you say so. And it's Dex, not Declan.*

"We've been looking for you since last year, actually. Way before your boyfriend reported you missing."

"What?"

The detective's lips turned up, like he'd scored a point. "Mr McCulloch's trafficking ring has been on our radar a long time. The team tracking his movements identified you as a potential victim sometime last autumn, but then you vanished. It was only by chance an officer in London cross-referenced Mr Wright's report with our database. Most wouldn't bother."

Mr Wright.

Seb.

Seb had reported him missing. The notion made Dex's head

spin. He wrapped his arm tighter round his knees, breathing in the scent of his clean clothes. Somehow, they smelled of Seb's bed... of him, and the scent grounded him, if only for a moment.

"Do you recognize this man, Declan?"

Dex glanced at the photo the older, sterner detective held out. The man had an Irish face, but he recognized little else. "No."

"Are you sure? Because you went missing from the Traveller camp in Hatfield not long after he was found dead in the woods."

Dex blinked. His blood ran cold. "What?"

"Tommy Smith. A dog walker found him in the woods with a bullet in his brain. We suspected Mr McCulloch and raided the site a few days later. We shut it down, but McCulloch was long gone, and so were you. Can you tell us where you went? How did you end up in London with Mr Wright? You know you were working illegally in the restaurant, don't you? Rick Wilson's been warned for that before. I'd hate to see him shut down."

"I didn't work there. I just helped out."

"Fair enough. That's not our concern just yet. Right now, we need to know who killed Tommy Smith. Can you tell us?"

Bastard. The question was simple enough, and the thinly veiled threat perfectly clear. *Tell us what we want or we'll fuck up the only real life you've ever had.*

Dex swallowed hard. His heart beat wildly in his chest. It was against Traveller lore to talk to the police. The vow of silence was sacred. The thought of breaking it filled him with an unease so deep his teeth itched, and yet he was considering it. Mikey was apparently dead, and Braden locked up. No one else would care enough to track him down, and perhaps if he gave the gorjers what they wanted, they'd let him be on his way.

He thought of Cora too. Tommy Smith meant nothing to him, but the elderly horse had been innocent, and her face still haunted his dreams.

"Excuse me, gentleman."

The new voice startled Dex. He looked up and met the gaze of a third detective—a clean-shaven man with scruffy brown hair. Scruffy brown hair he'd seen somewhere before.

"Keep your head down and your mouth shut, got it? They'll fuck you up if you fight them, and have you that way instead."

Dex clamped his hand over his mouth and shrank back on the bed. The policemen exchanged a few words, and the first two detectives left, leaving him alone with the gorjer john who'd brought him a bottle of scotch on that industrial estate in Hatfield.

Nausea rolled again as Dex tried to recall his name. John, Jim... no... George, that was it. He'd given him a pat on the back and a bottle of whiskey. *And then he left you for the others. Some fucking copper.*

George peered around the curtain, watching his colleagues depart. Then he slid nonchalantly into the bedside chair and grinned like he didn't have a care in the world. "Didn't expect to find you alive, mate. How the fuck did you manage that?"

Dex stared at him. "You're a copper."

"Yep. Been working undercover on your manor since the beginning of last year. Was counting on you to turn snitch. Fucked me right over when you legged it."

He's a copper. Dex said the words over and over in his head, but he couldn't match them with the smoky, dirty card game Braden had sold him to. The police were the enemy, of that he was certain, but they didn't do shit like George had done to him. Did they?

"Listen, I can't stay long. I just wanted you to know that whatever happens now, you're safe, okay? They're going to try and get you to turn snitch on McCulloch, but you don't need to. Braden's finished, he's done. They don't need you. They're just being greedy."

"Do they know you made me blow you?"

George leaned forward, his posture easy and confident. "No, but I had a remit to do whatever was needed to blend in. Think about it. If it wasn't me that night, it would've been someone else."

Dex's skin tingled... like ants were crawling all over his body. This was wrong, so fucking wrong, and he'd had enough. He wanted... needed Seb, and he needed to get the fuck out of this insane asylum. "I don't understand."

Dex's voice was a whisper, and George's half smile would've seemed kind in any other circumstances. "You don't need to. Just get your fella and go back to London. Do yourself a favour, kid. Forget where you came from."

GO AWAY. *Go away. Go away.*

"You were living with Mr Wright in London, is that correct?"

Dex opened his eyes with a heavy sigh. Creepy George was long gone, and the detectives too—back to wherever they came from, distinctly unimpressed with his renewed vow of silence. But he hadn't been alone for long. He'd barely put a foot on the shiny floor when their spot at the end of the bed had been filled.

The umpteenth new face was a woman—Elaine—a social worker who smelled like lemons and kept blowing her nose. "Declan," she prompted. "Your place of residence is Shackwell Lane, Dalston? With Seb?"

Seb. It felt like days since anyone had called him that. Mr Wright. Mr Sweeney. Declan. Who *were* these people?

"Or do you live at St. Mary's hostel in Stoke Newington?"

Dex scowled. Elaine, like the police, seemed to know more about him than he did himself. She knew the answers to her bone-head questions.

"Is that where you'd like to return? To the hostel? Or would you rather go home with Seb?"

"What's it to you?"

Elaine looked up, a small smile playing at her lips. "That's the first time you've spoken since I came in here. Is Mr Wright someone you would feel safe with?"

"Yes."

"He's here, you know. He'd like to take you home, if that's what you want."

Fuck off. People kept telling him that, but still no Seb. Perhaps they'd made it all up, and he had never been there at all. "Can I go now?"

"Soon. The police will want to know exactly where you're going, and I'd like to check in with you from time to time too."

"Why?"

"To monitor your welfare. Given your background and what you've been through, you're classified as a vulnerable adult. I'd like to make sure you're settled somewhere safe." Elaine held out a small white card. "Call me anytime. If things don't work out in London, I can help you find alternative housing."

"I don't have a phone."

"Not what I heard. Unpack the one you have under Seb's bed, turn it on, and program in this number."

Dex took the card and crumpled it in his fist. How did *she* know he'd stashed his few paltry belongings under Seb's bed? He glanced around for his shoes. *Whatever.* He'd heard enough. Seb wasn't here. He couldn't be, and without him, there was no reason to stay.

Elaine left. Dex took his chance and slipped around the curtain. A uniformed policeman stood at the end of the corridor. Dex turned and fled in the opposite direction. He came to a thick set of double doors, then another. Doors, doors, doors. He pushed through what felt like hundreds before he saw some that led outside.

The big glass doors lay at the far end of a large room. The room was lined with chairs, each one occupied by a pale-faced soul clutching a cardboard bowl or a bandaged limb. Blood roared in Dex's ears, but no one seemed to notice him loitering barefoot by a vending machine with his strange blue arm. He took a step forward, then another, and another, until he was running.

He darted across the room. Freedom was so close he could almost taste it. Someone shouted behind him, but the sound was muffled by Dex's pounding heart, and he didn't turn around. The doors opened as if on cue, and freezing air hit him like a truck. He ran on, following a trail lit only by lamps hidden in the bushes around the frosty car park. Somehow, he'd missed the day turning into a dark winter's night.

He ran and ran until the lights petered out and he found himself at the entrance to some kind of building site. He stared around the yard and sucked in laboured breaths, bent double with his uninjured hand on his knee. His blood slowed to a dull roar, but the quiet was worse. Defeat swept over him. He was out, he was free, but he had nowhere to go.

"Dex."

CHAPTER TWENTY-FIVE

"DEX."

Seb's tired voice brought Dex to his knees. Maybe this was it, the end he'd dreamed of. Perhaps if he lay down right here on the frosty tarmac, he'd go to sleep and never wake up.

Exhaustion washed over Dex. He swayed. Strong hands caught him and warm arms engulfed his whole body in a fierce embrace he'd feared he'd never feel again. The world as he knew it spun on its axis. Wetness dripped onto the back of his neck and a belt buckle dug into his hip. He hurt all over and his arm throbbed, but he didn't care. He buried his face in the sweetly scented planes of Seb's chiselled chest and let out a breath that left his limbs loose.

I missed you.

"Dex."

Seb murmured his name over and over and cradled him in his arms like he was made of glass. Dex's teeth chattered and violent shudders rattled his bones, but the shaking wasn't his own. Seb touched his face, his cheeks, and his lips. "Oh God, Dex. I thought… I thought you were dead."

Dex stared up at Seb, half-awed by the masculine beauty of his face and half-horrified by the bruising dark circles marring his magical eyes. He reached up and traced one. It hadn't been there before, had it? It seemed so long since he'd seen Seb's face, he wasn't sure.

"Dex, I'm going to move us, okay? Can you stand?"

Walked out here, didn't I? Dex scrambled to his unsteady feet, ignoring the persistent ache in his ribs. Seb followed suit and grabbed his hand. "Come on, let's get you back inside. We can talk in the warm."

Dex planted his feet on the ground like a stubborn horse. "No."

Seb glanced rapidly between Dex and the hospital doors. "You don't want to go in?"

Dex shook his head. Seb squeezed his hand, his expression torn. "It's cold out here, and you're just wearing a T-shirt. The doctors are looking for you too. They want to check your arm before they discharge you. I'm not going to make... shit." Seb inhaled a shaky breath. The tear tracks on his face gleamed in the murky light of the half moon. "I'm never going to make you do anything, you hear me? Just tell me what you want."

Dex took his hand from Seb and wrapped his good arm around himself. He wanted to climb inside Seb and never come out, but the words weren't there. Seb's gaze didn't waver... it never had, but Dex had to look away. He wasn't worthy of the emotion in Seb's eyes. He didn't deserve it.

Seb put his arm around Dex's shoulders, pulling him closer when he didn't resist. "There's a bench over there. Will you sit with me awhile?"

As if he could refuse. Seb led him to the bench beneath the flickering streetlight and eased him down to sit curled on Seb's lap, his head on his shoulder, as Seb brushed his fingers gently through his tangled hair.

Seb draped his coat around him, and for a while, they sat in a silence that seemed to swallow them up. A silence that consumed the time they'd spent apart like it had never happened at all. Periodically, one of them shivered, but Dex was too tired to figure out who. Instead, his mind wandered, drifting in and out of a strange doze that felt like an out-of-body experience.

Eventually, it became disconcerting. He flexed the fingers on his injured arm, using the pain to tie himself down to the world. Strapped into the steely blue cast, his fingers were pale and limp. He wondered if they'd ever feel the same as they did before.

"I'm sorry, Dex."

Dex tore his gaze from his arm. "What for?"

"For everything." Seb shrugged. "I'm so sorry this happened to you. I should've looked harder for you. I should've fought harder with the police."

"The police? What do you mean?"

Seb sighed before he seemed able to look back at Dex. "I reported you missing the morning after you disappeared, but the police in London wouldn't take me seriously. I couldn't tell them anything... fuck. I didn't even know your name. I had to go back twice before they let me file a report."

"How did you know I was lost?"

"You left your hat on the pavement. I picked it up, and I just knew something was wrong. I could accept that you might leave me... but I knew you loved the hat."

Seb grinned faintly, but Dex frowned. Didn't Seb know? Didn't he know Dex loved him to the moon and back? Like his ma used to tell him when the nights turned cold and the stars were their only friends? "What changed their minds?"

"Rick asked around the locals, and after a bit of persuasion, it turned out some old codgers in the snooker club saw someone getting thrown into the back of a van. They didn't give us much, but I knew it was you. I went back to the police station and refused to leave until they heard me out. A woman from CID walked past while I was giving the desk sergeant a hard time. She'd just read an e-mail from a force in Hertfordshire investigating the prosti—network at the site you came from."

Seb's slip was slight... a hesitation, a tremor in his voice he couldn't quite hide, but Dex heard it like he'd shouted it from the rooftops, and reality hit him deep in his belly.

He knows.

He sat up and pulled away from Seb, tearing himself from the embrace that made him feel whole. His breath stuck, but instead of panic, he felt hollow and lost.

He knows.

Seb caught Dex's arm. His grip was loose, but his eyes were stricken and wide. "What's the matter?"

Dex shrugged away. Seb's touch was a cruel trick. Too good to be true. "Why did you look for me? Why didn't you just leave me there?"

"I didn't know where 'there' was. I didn't know if you were dead or alive... or worse."

Worse. Yeah, this is definitely worse. "So?"

"So? So, what? You think I didn't give a shit? That the last two months meant nothing to me? Fuck's sake, Dex. You know me better than that, whether you want to or not. Goddamnit. I love the bones off you. Can't you tell?"

Dex snorted and shook his head. "Why would you love me? I'm a whore. I've always been a whore. It's who I am. You can't love someone like me."

"You're not a whore."

"I am."

"No, you're not. You're a young man who had his childhood stolen by a sick bastard who used him for his own gain. You didn't choose it. You were sold... like a commodity, and you weren't the only one. The police found human remains on that farm, Dex. The remains of murdered teenage boys—" Seb broke off and stared up at the sky. "I don't know what I would've done if the police had found your body."

Dex hauled himself to his feet and turned his back on Seb.

I'm just a whore.

"No, you're not," Seb said quietly. Dex blinked, unaware he'd spoken aloud. "You're not *just* anything. You can read, you can write. You're a chef, a friend, a lover. You know, the night you went missing, I was going to tell you I loved you and ask you to stay... stay with me, properly. Officially. With papers and shit, so you could earn real money and have a normal life."

"You wanted me to be *normal*?"

Seb sighed. "I wanted you to be *safe*. I didn't know about any of this, but I knew you were hiding from something, someone. I wanted to keep you safe... protect you from whatever you were so scared of. Fucked that right up, didn't I?"

"Not really. This is who I am."

"No, it's not." There was movement behind Dex, and Seb was suddenly right in front of him, his eyes fierce, as though he wanted to shake Dex's very soul. "*This* is something awful that happened to you. I know who you really are, and I love you more now than I did when you were taken from me."

How? How can you love me?

Seb closed the gap between them and took his face in his hands. "Dex, I love you, and I want you to come home with me, stay with me, and be happy with me for as long as you want to be, but it's your choice. You don't belong to me any more than you did to... anyone else. Whatever happens now is up to you."

Choice. It wasn't a word Dex knew well, and he only knew it at all because of the man holding him in such a gentle grip. There was no doubt in Dex's heart that he loved Seb... lived and breathed only for him, but could he be what Seb deserved in return? Could he even try?

Seb rubbed his cheek with the pad of his thumb. "Apparently you're quite the stable boy too. Someone on the site told the police you took care of the horses they found in the outbuildings."

"What?"

Dex snapped his eyes open. Seb stilled his thumb and studied Dex a moment. "The police raided the site months ago. They found some horses in an old shed. The RSPCA took them away."

"Where? Took them where?"

"Easy." Seb laid his palm flat on Dex's chest, like he could push his jumping heart back in his chest. "I don't know, exactly. Somewhere in Buckinghamshire, I think."

Dex slid from the bench, jarring his battered body. "Where's that?"

"Miles away. Dex, calm down. It's okay. We can look it up

when we get home. Maybe we can go see them when you're better."

"I want to see them now." The strength in his own voice surprised Dex, but he could hardly fathom the emotion building in his chest. Most of the horses were surely dead, but a few had been sound when he left. Robin, Lalla, and Ozzie. Maybe they'd survived long enough for the police to take them away.

Seb stood. He pulled his phone from his pocket and held it up to the light. For a moment, Dex feared he'd made him angry, and then Seb looked at him in a way that warmed him from the inside out, rushing through his veins like molten lava and healing every wound in its path.

"I'll make you a deal. Go inside and get discharged properly, and I'll take you wherever you want to go."

Dex stared up at him. "You'll take me to the horses?"

Seb smiled and kissed the very tip of his nose. "If that's what you want. What *do* you want, Dex?"

"I want to be with you."

CHAPTER TWENTY-SIX

Summer 2013

SEB TURNED the car onto the unsurfaced country lane. He pulled to a stop, but Dex was out and bounding up the dirt track before he'd engaged the handbrake. Dex loped up to the wooden fence and cleared it in a single leap. Seb grinned. Back in the city, he'd never noticed how agile Dex was, but now, seeing him hurdle a rickety old fence made him smile so hard his cheeks ached.

He shut off the car engine, content to sit back as Dex did his thing. He watched in wonder as Dex whistled, and the elderly horses in the field answered his soft call, ambling over to where he stood. It was the same every Monday. They'd sleep in, have sex and a lazy breakfast in bed, and then Seb would ask Dex what he wanted to do and it wouldn't be long before they were climbing in the car to drive the hour-long trip to Amersham. The staff at the rescue centre loved Dex, once they'd realised he wasn't going to steal the scruffy horses back, at least. They let him feed them, and they called him from time to time when one of them—Carric, maybe? Seb couldn't tell them apart—wasn't doing so well.

The whole thing was wonderful and heartbreaking, and Seb wanted to cry every time he saw Dex with his beloved horses. The similarities between them were too much. The horses had been locked in a shed, left to die, and Dex's own fate hadn't been all that different.

Seb shuddered, fighting the urge to let his mind wander to a darker place. Dex was safe and sound, feeding carrot tops to the horses in the fields, but the true horrors of what he'd been through haunted Seb. They never talked about it. Ever. Not since Seb had brought Dex home from the hospital. Dex because, well, who really knew, with Dex? He didn't talk much about anything unless he was drunk. And Seb? He didn't know how. What was he supposed to say? *Hey, Dex? Remember that slavery ring you were sold to when you were a child? The one that left you starved and half-dead on some deserted farmland? Yeah. Let's talk about that.*

Fat chance. No. Instead Seb paid a therapist to help Dex recover from a lifetime of abuse and watched from the sidelines as Dex slowly grew into a happy, healthy man. A man with real light in his eyes and flesh on his bones. A man who smiled like the sun.

That was enough for Seb. Dex's smile would always be enough.

Dex's physical affection helped too. Seb had expected Dex to shy away from sex after what he'd been through, but he hadn't. In fact, sometimes it seemed his ordeal had set him free in some way, like he'd separated his past from his present and never looked back.

It didn't happen that way for Seb. Sometimes, he looked at Dex and all he could see was the battered, broken shell he'd found huddled on the ground in a hospital car park. The police psychologists said Dex might suffer from flashbacks or bad dreams, and the nightmares came all right, just not to Dex. He slept like the dead every night, safe in Seb's arms while Seb lay sweating, imagining what could've happened if the police hadn't found Dex in the back of that van.

The police still came back from time to time, trying to persuade Dex to talk, but they always went away empty-handed. It was over for Dex. Done. And he wasn't going to break the only thing still tying him to where he came from. The Traveller vow of silence was something Seb would never understand, but over time, he'd come to accept there were many things he'd never know about Dex. Perhaps many things he didn't want to know, and maybe that was the point, the logic behind whatever twist of fate had brought Dex into his life. He couldn't change the wrongs of Dex's past, but he could instead help him make his future a life worth living.

Nice theory. Seb shook his head and opened his eyes just as Dex slid back into the car, his hair a mess, smelling of grass and hay.

"What are you shaking your head about?"

"Nothing. All present and correct?"

Dex glanced at the horses still milling by the fence. "Tauna has a sore leg. She needs some white willow bark."

"What's that?"

"Bark from a white willow tree." Dex shot Seb a look that made him feel like a fool. "It helps horses move better when they're old and lame."

"Where do you get that? From the vet?"

"Maybe, but there are probably a ton of willow trees down by the river. Can we go see?"

Seb suppressed a sigh. The question was innocent enough, but that Dex felt the need to ask got under his skin. Dex had trouble making decisions for himself, and it often didn't occur to him to try. Seb got out of the car and squinted south where the misfit stream of the River Misbourne lay. "Lead the way."

A FEW hours later, after far too much tramping through the mud for Seb's liking, they made their way back to the bustle of London. Dex had an extra shift at the restaurant, and Seb had plenty at home to keep him busy.

They had a quiet lunch together before Dex left for the evening service. Seb watched him disappear into the heady Dalston crowds from the balcony. A pesky amalgamation of worry and pride teased his heart. Dex had come home to him robbed of what little confidence he'd acquired before his old life snatched him back. It was returning, day by day, bolstered by the knowledge the man responsible would end his days in prison, but Seb still fretted.

How could he not, when the police had found the bones of a dozen young boys buried on that farm?

Stop it. Seb came back into himself with a jolt. He'd done that a lot recently—found himself lost in the past, dwelling on what could've been. He gave himself a shake and drifted back inside. If Dex could look forward, so could he.

Seb flopped on the sofa. The mischievous gaze of Dex's pet cat greeted him, and he eyed the scrawny tortoiseshell with suspicion. He loved cats, but the stray Dex had attached himself to was somewhat of a terrorist. Sweet and innocent one minute, then swinging from his neck by its claws the next.

Bloody thing should've come with an ASBO.

Seb cautiously petted the antisocial cat—*Jeanie*—and reached for his laptop. Dex had come back from his search for willow trees with a sweatshirt full of wild watercress, and it had given Seb an idea. Dex muddled along in the city because it didn't occur to him to do anything else, but his heart lay in the countryside, amongst the trees and the mud and the animals. Seb was a townie and he liked his creature comforts, but there had to be a way to bring the best bits of both together. There had to be, and he was determined to find it.

He figured he'd struck gold when the flat's buzzer sounded a little while later. He glanced at the clock. It was too early for Dex, and he had a key, anyway. He shut his laptop with a reluctant sigh and got up to investigate.

His sister's singsong voice greeted him through the intercom. He buzzed her in and wandered into the kitchen to put the kettle on and search out something sweet to keep her quiet. He loved Kelly to death, but she had a tendency to talk his ear off.

Lucky for him, Dex had made a killer Tottenham cake, and it was a while before Kelly got around to winding him up.

"Dex makes a better sponge than you," she said.

"You don't have to tell me that. Who do you think taught him?" Seb rolled his eyes, but Kelly's ribbing was pretty close to the truth. Dex was a good chef, a really good chef. His knife skills were far better than Seb's, and his lack of classical knowledge and training made his ideas unique. Sticky pear and chilli pudding. Who would've thought?

Kelly shoved the last bite of pink-iced cake in her mouth. "What are you doing this weekend?"

"What I do every weekend. Working."

"Don't be an arse." Kelly shot him a withering look. "I meant on Sunday. You finish at five on Sundays, don't you?"

Seb conceded her point with a nod. The early finish on Sundays was new, but since Rick had received an off-the-books warning from the police for letting Dex work without papers, he'd become more stringent about enforcing the rules. To adhere to a forty-eight-hour week, something had to give. For Seb and Dex, that meant Sunday nights and Thursday mornings were now their own.

Declan Sweeney.

Dex's full name still didn't quite seem real. Rick had helped Dex get the documents he needed to live and work in London. Without a birth certificate, it was a difficult process, and at times, Seb had worried it would never happen, but with the help of social services, it had all come together in the end. Not that it mattered much to Dex. Things Seb perceived as important often meant little to him.

"Are you even listening to me?"

Seb blinked at Kelly. "What are you wittering on about?"

"I was saying, brother dearest, are you and Dex going to come to Ezra's for a roast next week? Save you feeding yourselves after a weekend in the kitchen."

Seb hesitated. Dex got along fine with Kelly. She mothered him to death, and he let her, returning her affection in ways no one else would probably think of. Painstakingly handwriting thank-you notes for the nice things she did for him. Picking her wild-flowers from the fields near the horses. It was much like his rela-tionship with Bernie, only better, because Kelly was Seb's sister, and seeing them together just felt right.

Ezra, on the other hand.... They'd met up before, and Dex had seemed terrified of his forthright older brother.

"I don't know...."

Kelly raised an eyebrow. "What's up? You think Dex won't want to?"

"It's not that." And it wasn't. Dex would go anywhere Seb asked him to, and that was part of his problem—his ingrained instinct to do what he was told. "It's Ezra. I think he scares him. He seemed a little rattled when we all went to the zoo that time."

Kelly frowned, her shrewd gaze turning thoughtful. Rick aside, she was the only soul who knew what Dex had been through, and it had brought her and Seb closer together, bonded them around something horrific. "I don't think it was Ezra that scared Dex."

She let the statement hang, but her expression left Seb in no doubt that she had more to say. He gestured for her to go on.

"I think it was the cages and the clanging doors," Kelly said. "Didn't you notice how he jumped every time a keeper slammed a cage shut and locked it up? He looked like he'd seen a ghost."

Seb felt sick. The theory had never occurred to him, but it made sense. The police told them Dex had been held captive for most of his life, one way or another, and he'd been as jumpy as a cat the day they'd met his siblings at the London Zoo.

Kelly ruffled his hair. "Don't feel bad about it, Seb. These things are going to happen. You can't protect him from what happened, and he'll wind up hating you if you try. Let him be afraid of something and get over it in his own way. Don't coddle him."

Easy for her to say, and she left after that, leaving him with a jumbled pile of wisdom to dwell on.

He was still brooding in the dark when Dex arrived home a

little while later. The front door closed with a quiet click. Seb hauled his arse from the sofa and turned on a few lights. Dex was often content to grope around in the dark, but Seb was trying to train him out of it. He flipped on the kettle and met Dex in the hall.

"All right?"

"Yeah. Quiet night." Dex hung up his coat and lined his shoes up with Seb's. He looked dishevelled and tired, and wonderful.

Seb wanted to wrap his arms around him and never let go. Ever. "Want a cuppa?"

Dex thought for a moment. "After a shower?"

For once, Seb ignored the habitual uncertainty. "Go on. I'll meet you in bed."

They parted ways, Dex to the bathroom and him to shut up the rest of the flat before taking himself to bed. He crawled into bed and stared at the ceiling. The shower shut off, but it was a while before Dex crept up the stairs, and Seb knew he'd find the bathroom spotlessly clean come the morning.

Dex ghosted up the spiral staircase in just a pair of clean boxer shorts. It was August. The weather in London was muggy and warm, and even shy Dex had to concede to sleeping near enough nude. Didn't stop him burrowing under the covers like a cat, though. Dex loved their bed. In colder weather, it was hard to get him out. Not that Seb minded. Huddled in bed with Dex was his favourite place to be.

Dex slithered across the mattress and put his chin on Seb's chest. He didn't speak, but his soft smile said a thousand words.

Seb pushed Dex's coal-dark hair out of his face and felt a pang of longing for the halo of platinum locks he'd sported when they'd first met. He'd never quite understood the story behind them. "Tired?"

Dex nodded and closed his eyes, but he let his hands roam Seb's chest. His touch was light and lazy and drove Seb *insane*.

Seb shifted and drew in a shaky breath. "Feels nice."

"Nice?" Dex chuckled and brushed his thumb over Seb's nipple. "How about this?"

Seb moaned as the hot, wet heat of Dex's tongue explored every curve of muscle and flesh on his torso. His dick hardened, and he felt Dex thick and heavy against his leg.

He sat up, rolled them over, and pressed his lips to Dex's in a sweetly biting kiss. He ran his hands over Dex's smooth torso, still marvelling that, despite his ordeal, Dex didn't have a single scar on his flawless pale skin. Not a day went by when Seb couldn't recall the police flatly listing Dex's injuries from his time held captive on Braden McCulloch's derelict farm, but Seb tried to save those nightmares for when he was alone.

Dex whimpered and pushed at Seb's underwear. Seb let him have his way, and it wasn't long before they were both bare and moving together with a friction that consumed every nerve in Seb's body. He rolled them again, letting Dex call the shots. Sometimes, it helped his state of mind to know Dex was in control of their encounters. To know Dex was doing it because he wanted to… not because he lacked the ability to say no.

And sometimes, it just wasn't to be. Sometimes Dex said it all without saying a word. Dex rolled them again and pulled Seb over him, his intent and desire clear. *Take me. I'm yours.*

Seb slid careful fingers into Dex, ever mindful of his lover's fragile body. Dex said sex with Seb never hurt, but Seb watched him like a hawk, just to be sure. Two fingers became three. Dex arched his back and widened his legs. Sweat beaded his chest. Seb lubed his sheathed cock and eased inside him, watching and waiting for that magical moment when the discomfort of being filled gave way to all-encompassing pleasure.

"Oh."

Seb shuddered. Dex's breathy exclamation always hit him like a train… a train made from feathers and silk, with the bite of a snake. His dick pulsed, putting him right on the edge far too soon. He dropped his head into the crook of Dex's neck and grounded himself in all that was Dex. "You drive me bloody crazy, you know that?"

Dex shivered and flexed his hips. "You talk too much."

Seb took the hint and let the natural current between them

take over. Their coupling was slow and sweet, belying the crazy desire that sometimes overcame them. Beneath him, Dex writhed and moaned, crying out when release hit him.

Seb watched him through hooded eyes, feeling his own climax sweep over him like a soft summer wave. He loved having sex like this, and he knew, given the chance, that he could watch Dex like this forever.

CHAPTER TWENTY-SEVEN

SEB OBSERVED from the dessert counter as Dex incorporated the tepid water, yeast, and sugar into the mound of seasoned flour and worked it into smooth, elastic dough. He loved watching Dex make bread. The industrial mixer and dough hook were just a few feet away, but kneading the dough by hand was good for Dex's healed wrist, and he seemed to enjoy it.

Lucky, because the next day was a bank holiday, and Rick had decided the restaurant needed to contribute a stall to the local carnival. Seb had been charged with stocking and manning it, and it hadn't taken much to rope Dex into helping. Not that Dex knew about the manning part. Seb was saving that bomb for the following morning, hoping Dex would be too shell-shocked by the predawn start to protest too much.

Seb wrapped up his last batch of scones and wandered over to the trays of bread dough Dex had set up to proof overnight. "What are you putting in that one?"

Dex pointed to a muslin-wrapped bundle. "The wild rosemary we found by the stream last week."

"*You* found," Seb said. "I was too busy trying not to fall in."

Dex laughed. Over the summer, they'd spent most of their free time hiking through the woods near the farm where Dex's elderly horses lived, and Seb had fast learned Dex had a huge knowledge of the wildlife and countryside. Herbs, berries, poisonous plants. The trees and the creatures that lived among them. It was startling, to Seb at least, and didn't quite match up with his grimly imagined images of Dex's childhood.

It also underlined his ongoing worry that maybe an inner-city kitchen wasn't the best place for Dex. He worked hard, and he'd tackled every section in the kitchen, but he'd yet to find the role that suited him best. Perhaps there wasn't one. Perhaps it was time for a change.

THE NEXT day dawned warm and bright. Seb dragged Dex out of bed at dawn, and they spent the morning cooking up a storm. By the time midday came around, they had a trestle table overflowing with breads, cakes, and jars of jam made from Dex's secret stash of wild strawberries.

Seb hustled Dex out of the kitchen to see the fruits of their labour. "What do you think? Looks good, eh?"

Dex nodded, his reactions as muted as ever. "Are we going home now?"

"Nope. Who do you think is going to sell all this?"

"Um, Bernie?"

Seb chuckled. "You wish. Go put a clean jacket on and get your arse back out here."

Dex's expression said it all, but it wasn't his way to protest, and by the time he slunk outside a little while later, Seb was hard at work selling their wares. Years of fronting the family fudge shop meant the patter came easy to him, but it wasn't long before he realised Dex had hidden himself behind him.

Not today.

Seb handed an elderly woman her change and pulled off his bandana. "Hold the fort, will you? I'll be back in a minute."

Dex looked startled. "Where are you going?"

"Inside. I'll be back."

"Why?"

"Does it matter?"

Dex opened his mouth and shut it again. Seb punched his shoulder. "You know the prices. The change is in the tin."

He slipped away without giving Dex a chance to respond, effectively abandoning him on the stall. Cruel? Maybe, maybe not. Dex had worked a hair-braiding stall in Padstow all by himself, handling money and communicating with the outside world. It was all about confidence, and he would never regain it hiding behind Seb.

Seb loitered in the kitchen awhile before he deemed it safe to take a peek. What he saw when he did warmed his bones.

Bernie joined him at the back door. She followed his gaze, watching as Dex sold the last of his rosemary loaves to a burly Afro-Caribbean man, and nodded, needing no explanation. "He's changing every day," she said. "I'm so proud of him."

Seb said nothing, constrained by the lump in his throat, but it was a sentiment he shared with every fibber of his being. Dex was a stone heavier than he'd ever been, and his smile grew every time it appeared on his face.

Yeah. Life was good.

Seb let his experiment run its course and rejoined Dex at the stall a little while later. Dex was less than impressed. "I'm not a mute, you know, and I'm not stupid. I had to take the fares from people at the bumper cars on the fairgrounds."

Fairgrounds. Seb absorbed the snippet of information and enjoyed the rare moment of assertiveness from Dex. With his unfathomable grey eyes and surly pout, cross Dex was sexy as hell.

It was early evening by the time they called it a day. They walked home in high spirits, helped along by the pints of free cider Rick had passed their way all day.

They stumbled through the front door. Dex tripped over his feet, laughing, his eyes bright, no longer the sullen vagrant Seb had met on the seafront, but not the broken shadow his tormentor had left him either. This was a new Dex. Perhaps the real Dex, the Dex who had his whole life ahead of him, full of hope and promise and all the love he deserved.

Seb pulled him close, enveloping him in a tight hug that seemed to take Dex by surprise. Seb ignored his bemused gaze and kissed him with all he had.

Dex's response stopped him in his tracks. Often, when they kissed, Dex fell pliant in Seb's arms, almost melting into him like liquid silver, but, conversely, sometimes he stiffened, as though the thrill of being kissed hit him too hard. He did neither of those things now. Now he responded with a spirit that had Seb stumbling until his back hit the wall.

Seb broke away, breathless. Dex stared back at him, his chest heaving. He looked like he wanted to say something, but nothing came out, and the longer they gazed at each other, the more heated and heavy the air became.

Dex touched Seb's face, his eyes wide with wonder, like he'd never touched him before. "I feel weird today."

Seb absorbed the sensation of Dex pressed against the entire length of his body. "Weird?"

Dex shrugged. "Yeah. Like I need... something."

"Something from me?"

Dex thought on it a moment, then shook his head. "No. More like something *for* you."

"For me?" A tremor of anticipation rushed through Seb. He had an idea what Dex was trying to say, even if Dex didn't know it himself. "Do I need to take my shoes off?"

His shaky attempt at humour seemed to remind Dex they'd barely gotten through the door. Dex blinked and stepped back. He toed off his shoes and laid them deliberately on the rack by the door.

Seb watched, knowing whatever was going on in Dex's mind couldn't be forced. "Dex?"

Dex turned to face him, wresting with something only he knew. "I want to do what you want... that thing you don't want to ask me for, but I need you to tell me it'll be okay if I can't do it."

He wants to top? Seb considered his options. He was versatile, and he'd bottomed for all his partners before Dex, but Dex had never topped for anyone. He'd never had the choice. "You need to tell me what you want, so I know we're thinking about the same thing."

Calling Dex's bluff was a gamble, and one that didn't always pay off. Often, he shrugged and walked away before Seb had any clue what he was trying to say.

Dex stepped closer, putting himself back in Seb's personal space. "I want you to feel like I do."

I want you to love me.

"I do."

Seb blinked. "What?"

"I do love you, Seb."

It was all Seb needed to hear. It was all he'd *ever* needed to hear. He took Dex's face in his hands and pressed their foreheads together. "Come upstairs."

They fell into bed, Seb on his back and Dex over him, covering him and consuming him in ways that belied his smaller, leaner frame. Their clothes disappeared. Sweat, heat, and friction. Dex didn't falter until his condom-sheathed cock was with a hair-breadth of where Seb wanted it most.

Dex pulled away, panting. "I don't know how."

Seb tugged him back, widening his legs and creating a cradle for Dex between his thighs. "Yes, you do. Do what you feel, and I'll feel it too."

Dex dropped his hands on either side of Seb's head. The head of his dick nudged against Seb, rubbing, pressing, teasing. "I don't know how you feel."

Seb gripped Dex's chin and held his gaze as he raised his hips, taking Dex inside him in a gently punishing slide. "Yes. You. Do."

Dex bit his lip and thrust, his eyes rolling back in his head as Seb's body clamped down around him. "Do you love me?"

"Yes." Seb shuddered. He'd once believed Dex was no more

than a brief summer rain… a ghostlike dream that came around once in a lifetime. Now, with Dex filling him and stretching him until he felt his heart would burst… now it was clear Dex was the sky, and the ocean, and everything to him no one else had ever been.

Above him, Dex groaned, deep and low, and thrust his hips in a rhythm that fast became something primal. Seb closed his eyes and steadied himself on the wall behind him. Dex had a thick dick, but more than that, his heart was huge, and each stabbing dig of his cock set Seb on fire.

Seb felt like the intensity would shatter his body. His heart raced and his breathing became rapid and sharp. He forced his eyes open and found Dex watching him, his face a mirror image of what Seb felt every time they came together in bed: love, life, and a giddy exhilaration that knew no bounds.

Dex rose up on his knees, drawing one of Seb's legs to his chest to anchor himself as the pace of his thrusts grew in confidence.

Seb braced himself for the increase in pressure, took himself in hand, and let the carnal pleasure of Dex's cock inside him take over. His faculties left him one by one. Coherent thought and speech, his sight, all seared white. He arched his back and moaned, reaching out blindly for any part of Dex he could reach.

Dex grasped his hand and thrust once, twice, three times, and then pulsing warmth filled the space where they were joined.

Seb came with a sharp cry, spilling onto his belly. Elation filled him. Elation and something just… more. He opened his eyes to find Dex's face inches from his, and all at once, he felt the missing link between them become whole.

He pushed Dex's sweat-dampened hair away from his face, sucking in ragged breaths until he could speak. "Will you come somewhere with me tomorrow?"

A sleepy, sated smile graced Dex's beautiful face. "Of course."

DEX SPUN a slow circle in the dilapidated farmyard, his face a picture of bemused confusion. "I don't understand," he said. "There's nothing here."

Seb rolled his eyes, trying to tame the childlike excitement threatening to bubble out of his chest. The excitement had been building since they'd climbed into the car and driven the forty-mile trip out of London. He grasped Dex's shoulders and turned him back to the dilapidated farmhouse. "Not yet, but I'm hoping we can change that."

"Change it how?"

"I want to buy it." Seb pointed to the house. "That would be the restaurant. We'd live above it." He gestured to the woods surrounding the farm. "We could get local ingredients from the woods. Meat from the farm down the road. Grow our own herbs and veg." He turned Dex again and pointed to a cluster of outbuildings. "We could even keep a couple of those scraggly old nags you love so much."

"Horses?"

"If you want."

Dex was silent, and Seb held his breath, under no illusions that asking Dex to give up the newfound security of his life in London wasn't huge. His weekly wage was nothing to Seb, but to Dex, it was everything. The most he'd ever had.

"You'd be my boss."

"Not necessarily. You want to rescue horses, right? Like the place Tauna and Carric live?"

Dex nodded. He'd made no secret of his fascination with the farms that took in animals most sane people would have destroyed. "So?"

"So, you could work in the restaurant to pay for the horses. Help me source ingredients from the wild. Hell, Dex, you can do whatever you want. You don't have to work here at all."

Dex shook his head. "No. I like it here, I just... I don't know what that means."

"Is it because I'd own the building? Because that's all it is. Metal and dust. I'd give you half if I thought you'd let me."

194

Dex smiled, and Seb felt a flutter of hope in his heart. "I know you would," Dex said. "But I don't need you to. I just want to be where you are."

"That could be here. If you want. You really like it?"

Dex looked around and his grin split his beautiful face in half. "I do. I love it, and I love you too… more than that."

Seb's heart beat a stampede in his chest. "More than that, eh?"

Dex stepped into his arms like he'd been there all along… like there'd never been a world where they weren't together. "To the moon and back."

NEWSLETTER

Get a free story!

For the most up to date news and free books, subscribe to my newsletter HERE.

This is a zero spam zone. Maximum number of emails you will receive is one per month.

PATREON

Not ready to let go of Seb and Dex? Or looking for sneak peeks at future books in the series? Alternative POVs, outtakes, and missing moments from **all** Garrett's books can be found on her Patreon site. Misfits, Slide, Strays…the works. Because you know what? Garrett wasn't ready to let her boys go either.

Pledges start from as little as $2, and all content is available at the lowest tier.

ABOUT GARRETT LEIGH

Bonus Material available for all books on Garrett's Patreon account. Includes short stories from Misfits, Slide, Strays, What Remains, Dream, and much more. Sign up here: https://www.patreon.com/garrettleigh

Facebook Fan Group, Garrett's Den... https://www.facebook.com/groups/garre...

Garrett Leigh is an award-winning British writer, cover artist, and book designer. Her debut novel, Slide, won Best Bisexual Debut at the 2014 Rainbow Book Awards, and her polyamorous novel, Misfits was a finalist in the 2016 LAMBDA awards, and was again a finalist in 2017 with Rented Heart.

In 2017, she won the EPIC award in contemporary romance with her military novel, Between Ghosts, and the contemporary romance category in the Bisexual Book Awards with her novel What Remains.

When not writing, Garrett can generally be found procrastinating on Twitter, cooking up a storm, or sitting on her behind doing as little as possible, all the while shouting at her menagerie of children and animals and attempting to tame her unruly and wonderful FOX.

Garrett is also an award winning cover artist, taking the silver medal at the Benjamin Franklin Book Awards in 2016. She designs for various publishing houses and independent authors at blackjazzdesign.com, and co-owns the specialist stock site moonstock-photography.com

Connect with Garrett
www.garrettleigh.com

ALSO BY GARRETT LEIGH

Kiss Me Again

Lucky

Cash

Jude

Slide

Rare

Circle

Misfits

Strays

Dream

Whisper

Believe

Crossroads

Bullet

Bones

Bold

House of Cards

Junkyard Heart

Rented Heart

Soul to Keep

My Mate Jack

Lucky Man

Finding Home

Only Love

Heart

What Remains

What Matters

Between Ghosts